Madison Julius Cawein

Poems of Nature and Love

Madison Julius Cawein

Poems of Nature and Love

ISBN/EAN: 9783337408114

Printed in Europe, USA, Canada, Australia, Japan

Cover: Foto ©Andreas Hilbeck / pixelio.de

More available books at **www.hansebooks.com**

POEMS

OF

NATURE AND LOVE

BY

MADISON CAWEIN

G. P. PUTNAM'S SONS

NEW YORK
27 West Twenty-third St.

LONDON
24 Bedford St., Strand

The Knickerbocker Press

1893

Printed and Bound by
The Knickerbocker Press, New York
G. P. PUTNAM'S SONS

Under the present title are included selections from two former volumes, *Accolon of Gaul*, and *Lyrics and Idyls*. Such poems only as appeared to the author's judgment worthiest of retention have been retained. In the selection of these he has endeavored to exercise a critical discrimination and, to the best of his ability, to correct or expunge the frequent obscurity, superfluity, and exaggerated expression of the earlier works. Many of the poems have been partially, several entirely, rewritten.

TO

JOAQUIN MILLER

How shall I greet him—him who seems
  To me the worthiest of our singers?
As one who hears Sierra streams,
  And, gazing under arching fingers,
Feels all the eagle feels that screams,
  The savage dreams, what time he lingers?

Son of the West, out of the West
  We heard thee sing,—who still allurest,—
A land where God sits manifest,
  A land where man stands freest, surest;
A land, the noblest and the best,
  The loveliest and purest.

Wild hast thou sung, as some strange bird
  On golden cliffs, and winds that glistened,
And seas and stars and men have heard—
  And one, whose soul cried out and listened,
He sends his young, unworthy word
  To thee the Master's word hath christened.

CONTENTS.

REVERY.

What ogive gates from gold of Ophir wrought,
  What walls of marble, whiter than a rose,
What towers of crystal, for the eyes of thought,
  Hast builded on far Islands of Repose!

WHERE castled peaks and templed cliffs and
      vales
  Cloud — like convulsive sunsets—shores that
      dream,
Myrrh-fragrant, over siren seas whose sails
  Gleam white as lilies on a lilied stream,
Long have I dreamed! In gardens towards the sea,
  Down arcades of some sea-sad colonnade
    Of wreathen sculpture, long have walked with
        thought,
To bend, in shadowy attitude, the knee
  Before the shrine of Beauty that must fade
    And leave no memory of the mind that wrought.

Who hath beheld thy caverns where, in heaps,
  The wines of Lethe and Love's-witchery,
In sealéd amphoræ a Sibyl keeps,
  World-old, forever guarded secretly!—

No wine of Xeres or of Syracuse !
   No fine Falernian and no vile Sabine !—
      The stolen fire of a demigod,
Whose bubbled purple goddess feet did bruise
   From crusted vats of vintage, where the green
      Flames with wild poppies, on the Samian sod.

Oh, for the deep enchantment of one draught !
   The reckless ecstasy of classic earth !—
With godlike eyes to laugh as gods have laughed
   In eyes of mortal brown, a breezy mirth
Of deity delirious with desire !
   To breathe the dropping roses of the shrines,
      The splashing wine-libation and the blood,
And all the young priest's dreaming ! To inspire
   My eager soul with beauty, till it shines
      An utt'rance of life's loftier brotherhood !

So would I slumber in the old-world shades,
   And Poesy should touch me, as the bold
Wild-bees the virgin lilies of the glades,
   Barbaric with the pulpy-kerneled gold :
And feel the glory of the golden-age
   Less godly than my purpose, strong to dare
      Death with the pure, immortal lips of love :
Less lovely than my soul's ideal rage
   To mate itself with Music, and declare
      Itself part-meaning of the stars above.

SUMMER.

I.

THOU sit'st among the sunny silences
    Of passive hills and woodland majesties,
Thou utterance of all calm melodies,
Thou lutanist of Earth's most fecund lute,—
        Where no false note intrudes
To mar the silent music,—foot by foot
Playing broad fields ripe, orchards and deep woods,
        In song similitudes
        Of flower and seed and fruit.

II.

So have I heard thee in some sensuous air
Bewitch the wide wheat-acres everywhere
To imitated gold of thy rich hair :
The peach, by thy red lips' delicious trouble,
        Blown into gradual dyes
Of crimson ; with glad interludes to double—
Dark-blue with fervid influence of thine eyes—
        The grapes' rotundities
        Bubble by purple bubble.

III.

Deliberate uttered into life intense,
Out of thy mouth's melodious eloquence

Beauty evolves its just pre-eminence :
The lily, from some pensive-smitten chord
      Drawing significance
Of purity, a visible hush stands ; starred
With splendor, from thy passionate utterance,
      The rose writes its romance
      In blushing word on word.

IV.

As star by star day harps in evening,
The inspiration of all things that sing
Is in thy hands and from their touch takes wing :
All brooks, all birds,—no similar songs can sate,—
      All wings, the wind and rain,
Hoarse frogs and insects, singing rathe and late,
Thy sympathies inspire, and yet remain
      Patient to invigorate
      With rest life's toiling brain.

V.

And as the night, like some mysterious rune,
Its beauty makes emphatic with the moon,
Thou lutest us no immaterial tune :
But where hushed music haunts the cane and corn,
      And where the thick leaves throng,
Earth's awful avatar,—in whom is born
Thy own vast spirit,—labors all night long
      With growth, assuring morn
      Assumes like onward song.

GARGAPHIE.

" Succinctæ sacra Dianæ."—Ovid.

I.

THERE the ragged sunlight lay
  Tawny on thick ferns and gray
    On dark waters : dimmer,
Lone and deep, the cypress grove
Shadowed whisperings and wove
Braided lights, like those that love
On the pearl plumes of a dove
    Pale to gleam and glimmer.

II.

There centennial pine and oak
Into stormy utterance broke :
    Hollow rocks gloomed, slanting,
Echoing in dim arcade,
Looming with loose moss, that made
Sunshine streaks in tatters laid :
Oft a wild hart, hunt-afrayed,
    Plunged the water, panting.

III.

Poppies of a sleepy gold
Mooned the gold-green twilights rolled
    Down its vistas, making
Fuzzy puffs of flame.   And pale
Stole the dim deer down the vale.
And the haunting nightingale
Throbbed not near—the olden tale
    All its hurt heart breaking.

IV.

There the hazy serpolet,
Dewy cistus, blooming wet,
    Blushed on bank and boulder ;
There the cyclamen, as wan
As faint footprints of the Dawn,
Carpeted the spotted lawn :
There the nude nymph, dripping drawn,
    Basked a peachy shoulder.

V.

In the citrine shadows there
What tall presences and fair,
    White and godly gracious,—
Hidden where the rock-rose grew,—
Watched through eyeballs of the dew,
Or from sounding oaks ! and knew
All the mystery of blue
    Heaven, vaulted spacious !

VI.

Guarded that Bœotian
Valley so no foot of man
    Soiled its silence holy
With profaning tread—save one,
The Hyantian : Actæon,
He beheld . . . What god might shun
Fate, Diana's wrath called down,
    With what magic moly !—

VII.

Lost it lies ; like one who sleeps
In serene enchantment ; keeps
    Beautiful in beamy
Beauty of the flowers that be
Wisdom's ; hope, its high stars see,
Near in fountains ; deity,
In wise wind-words of each tree—
    Gargaphie the dreamy.

BENEATH THE BEECHES.

I.

I LONG, oh long to lie
  'Neath beechen branches, twisted
Green 'twixt the summer sky;
The woodland shadows nigh—
Brown dryads sunbeam-wristed :—
The live-long day to dream
Beside a wildwood stream.

II.

I long, oh long to hear
The claustral forest's breathings,
Sounds soothing to the ear;
The yellow-hammer near,
Beam-bright, thrid wild-vine wreathings :
The live-long day to cross
Slow o'er the nut-strewn moss.

III.

I long, oh long to see
The nesting red-bird singing

Glad on the wood-rose tree ;
To watch the breezy bee,
Half in the wildflower, swinging :
God's live-long day to pass
Deep in cool forest grass.

IV.

Oh you, so builded in
With mart and booth and steeple,
Brick alley-ways of Sin,
What hope for you to win
Ways free of pelf and people !
Ways of the leaf and root
And soft Mygdonian flute !

THE BRUSH-SPARROW.

I.

E RE wild-haws, looming in the glooms,
 Build bolted drifts of breezy blooms ;
And in the whistling hollow there
The red-bud bends as brown and bare
As buxom Roxy's up-stripped arm ;
From some gray hickory or larch,
Sighed o'er the sodden meads of March,
The sad heart thrills and reddens warm
To hear you braving the rough storm,
Frail courier of green-gathering powers :
Rebelling sap in trees and flowers ;
Love's minister come heralding—
O sweet saint-voice among bleak bowers !
O brown-red pursuivant of Spring !

II.

'' Moan '' sob the woodland cascades still
Down bloomless ledges of the hill ;
And gray, gaunt clouds like harpies hang
In harpy heavens, and swoop and clang

Sharp beaks and talons of the wind :
Black scowl the forests, and unkind
The far fields as the near : while song
Seems murdered and all beauty, wrong.
One weak frog only in the thaw
Of spawny pools wakes cold and raw,
Expires a melancholy bass
And stops as if bewildered : then
Along the frowning wood again,
Flung in the thin wind's vulture face,
From woolly tassels of the proud
Red-bannered maples, long and loud,
"*Her Grace ! her Grace ! her Grace !*"

III.

Her Grace ! her Grace ! her Grace !—
Climbs beautiful and sunny-browed
Up, up the kindling hills and wakes
Blue berries in the berry brakes :
With fragrant flakes, that blow and bleach,
Deep-powders smothered quince and peach :
Eyes dogwoods with a thousand eyes :
Teaches each sod how to be wise
With twenty wildflowers to one weed :
And kisses germs that they may seed.
In purest purple and sweet white
Treads up the happier hills of light,
Bloom, cloudy-borne, song in her hair
And balm and beam of odorous air :

Winds, her retainers ; and the rains
Her yeomen strong that sweep the plains :
Her scarlet knights of dawn, and gold
Of eve, her panoply unfold :
Her herald tabarded behold !
Awake to greet ! prepare to sing !
She comes, the darling Duchess, Spring !

THE OLD FARM.

DORMERED and verandahed, cool,
  Locust-girdled on the hill,
Stained with weather-wear and full
  Of weird whispers, at the will
Of the sad wind's rise or lull ;

I remember, it stood there
  Brown above the woodland ; deep
In a scent of lavender,
  With slow shadows locked in sleep
And the warm light everywhere.

I remember how the spring,
  Liberal-lapped, bewildered its
Squares of orchard, murmuring
  Kissed with budded puffs and bits,
Where the wood-thrush came to sing.

Barefoot so at first she trod,
  A pale beggar-maid, adown
The quaint quiet, till the god
  With the seen sun for a crown
And the firmament for rod,

Graced her nobly, wedding her—
  Her Cophetua.   And so
All the hill, one breathing blur,
  Burst in blossom, where the glow
And the peach-sweet fragrance were.

Seckel, blackheart palpitant
  Rained their bleaching strays ; and white
Bulged the damson bent a-slant ;
  Russet-tree and romanite
Seemed beneath deep drifts to pant.

And it stood there, brown and gray,
  In the bee-boom and the bloom,
In the murmur and the day,
  In the passion and perfume,
Grave as age among the gay.

Good as laughter romped the clear,
  Boyish voices round its walls ;
Rare wild-roses were the dear
  Girlish faces in its halls,
Music-haunted all the year.

Far before it meadows full
  Of green pennyroyal sank ;
Clover dots, like bits of wool
  Pinched from lambs ; and now a bank
Of wild color ; and the cool

Brown-blue shadows undefined
Of the clouds rolled overhead—
Curdled mists that kept the wind
Fresh with rain and comforted
With soft songs forever kind.

Where in mint and gypsy-lily
Ran the rocky brook away,
Musical among the hilly
Solitudes,—its flashing spray
Sunlight-soft or forest-stilly ;—

Buried in thick sassafras,
Half-way up the wooded hill,
Moved some cowbell's muffled brass ;
And the ruined water-mill
Loomed half-hid in cane and grass.

I remember—stands it yet
On the hilltop, in the musk
Of damp meads, while violet
Deepens all the dreaming dusk,
And the locust-trees hang wet

With the dew ? while, far and low,
One long tear of scarlet gashes,
Tattered, the broad primrose glow
Westward, and in weakest splashes
Lilac stars the heavens sow ?

Sleeps it still among its roses,
  Red and yellow, while the choir
Of the lonesome insects dozes?
  And the white moon, drifting higher,
Brightens and the darkness closes—
Sleeps it still among its roses?

THE BRIDLE-PATH.

I.

THROUGH meadows of the iron-weeds,
   Whose purple blooms flash, slipping
Twice-twinkling drops of dewy beads,
The thin path twists and winding leads
   Through woodland hollows dripping ;
Down to a creek with bedded reeds ;
On to the lilied dam that feeds
The mill, whose wheel through willow-bredes
   Winks, the white water whipping.

II.

It wends through meads of mint and brush
   Where silvery seeds sink drowsy,
Or sail along the heatful hush ;
Past where the bobwhite in the bush
   Has built a nest, and frowsy
Hides calling clear. A split through crush
Of crowded saplings, low and lush ;
A seam by pools of flag and rush
   Where blows the brier-rose blowsy.

2

III.

Across the ragweed fallow-lot,
    Whose low-rail fence encumbers
The dense-packed berries ripening hot ;
Where on the summer, one far spot
    Of gray, the gray hawk slumbers.
Then in the greenwood where the rot
Of leaves and loam smells cool ; and shot
With dotting dark the touch-me-not
    Swings curling horns in numbers.

IV.

Around brown rocks that bulge and lie
    Deep in damp ferns and mosses,—
Like giants, each lounged on his thigh
To watch some forest quarry die,—
    The path toils steep ; then crosses
A bramble-bridge ; up-whirring nigh
A wood-dove startles, 'thwart the sky
A jarring light : and babbling by
    The brook its diamonds tosses.

V.

Ho ! through the wildwood then we go
    In pulse of shade and singing ;
Where pale-pink sorrel-grasses grow ;
The vari-colored toadstools sow

And swell the soil, bestringing
The red-oak's roots. Where, swinging low
Their green burs, limbs rub when each slow,
Faint forest wind sounds. Fresh the flow
  Of hidden waters ringing.

VI.

While far away among the cane,
  Or spice-bush belts, the tinkle
Of one stray bell drifts yet again,
Lost near some lone and leafy lane
  Where smooth the red ruts wrinkle . . .
Now up the sky a grayish stain
Spreads smoky blue. A hint of rain.
The sun is hid. Hard down the grain
  A gust dents ; and a sprinkle

VII.

Has drilled the dimpled dust. Hark !—one
  Big mouthful of the thunder—
And, scurrying with the dust, we run
Into a whiff of hay and sun,
  Of cribs and barns ; and under
The martin-builded eaves,—where dun
The sparrows house with fuss and fun,—
" Will it be done soon as begun ?"
  We wonder and we wonder.

VIII.

A crashing wedge of stormy light
　Vibrating blinds, and dashes
A monster elm to splinters quite ;
A hush, then rushing rain that white
　The tumbled straw-stack lashes.　. .
The rain is over.　Left and right
Foregathering gales of green delight,
Fresh rain scents of each wood and height
　Where each blade drips and flashes.

IX.

A ghostly gold burns slowly through
　The crumbled clouds ; and woven
From rainy rose to rainy blue
A dim pearl-dotting as of dew
　Dies into trembling doven.
High-buoyed in rack now one or two
Slight stars shine white—the pirate clew
To night's rich hoard.—The west 's a hue
　Of bruised pomegranate cloven.

A GRAY DAY.

I.

L ONG volleys of wind and of rain,
    And the rain on the drizzled pane,
And the dusk comes chill and murk ;
But on yesterday's eve I know
How a new moon's thorn-like bow
Stabbed rosy through gold and through glow,
    Like a rich, barbaric dirk.

II.

The throats of the snapdragons,—
Cool-colored like dewiest dawns
    That a healthy yellow paints,—
Are filled with a sweet rain fine
Of a jaunty, jubilant shine,
A faery vat of rare wine,
    That the honey thinly taints.

III.

Dabbled the poppies shrink,
And the coxcomb and the pink ;
    And the candytuft's damp crown
Droops dribbled, low bowed i' the wet ;

Long counters of mignonette
Little musk-sacks open let,
　From the shelves o' the dew dragged down.

IV.

Stretched taunt on the blades of grass,　　•
A gossamer-fibered glass,
　That the garden-spider spun,
The web, where the round rain clings
In its middle sagging, swings—
A hammock for elfin things
　When the stars succeed the sun.

V.

And, mark, where the pale gourd grows
As high as the climbing rose,
　How the tiger-moth is pressed
To the wide leaf's under side.—
And I know where the red wasps hide,
And the brown bees,—that defied
　The first strong gusts,—distressed.

VI.

Yet I feel that the gray will blow
Aside for an afterglow ;
　And the wind, on a sudden, toss
Drenched boughs to a pattering show'r
Athwart the red dusk in a glow'r,
Big drops heard hard on each flow'r,
　On the grass and the flowering moss.

VII.

And then for a minute, may be,—
A pearl—hollow-worn—of the sea,—
  A glimmer of moon will smile ;
Cool stars rinsed clean o' the dusk ;
A freshness of gathering musk
O'er the showery lawns, as brusque
  As spice from an Indian Isle.

THE MOOD O' THE EARTH.

MY heart is high, is high, my dear,
  As the wind in the wood that blows ;
My heart is high with a mood that 's cheer,
  And burns like a sun-blown rose.

My heart is high, my dear, my dear,
  And the heaven's deep skies are blue ;
My heart goes out to the passionate year,
  As glad as a cloud with dew.

My heart, my heart is high, my sweet,
  And wild as the smell o' the wood,
That gusts i' the breeze with a pulse of heat,
  Mad heat that beats like a blood.

My heart is high ; and it guides my feet
  Where the sense of summer is full ;
A sense of summer—full fields of wheat,
  Full forests the swift creeks cool.

My heart is one, is one, my heart,
  With the brown bee's heart that sinks
And sounds i' the flowers that dip and part
  To his dusty body that drinks.

My heart is high, my heart, my heart !
　Sing ! sing again, O good, gray bird !
That I may get that lilt by heart,
　And fit each note with a word.

God's saints !　I tread the air, my dear !
　Am one with the hoiden wind ;
And the stars that stare I swear, my dear,
　Right soon in my hair I 'll find.—

To live high up a life of mist,
　With the white things in white skies,—
With their limbs of pearl and of amethyst,—
　Who laugh blue, humorous eyes !

To creep and to suck, like an elfin thing,
　In the aching heart of a rose ;
In the bluebell's ear to cling and swing
　And whisper what no one knows !

To live on wild honey as fresh as thin
　As the rain that 's left in a flower !
And roll out golden from toe to chin
　In the god-flower's Danaë shower !

Or free, full-throated, bend back the throat,
　With a vigorous look at the blue,
And sing, and sing with a staunch wild note,
　Like the thrush there ere it flew.

God's life ! the blood o' the Earth is mine !
And the mood o' the Earth I 'll take,
And brim my soul with her wonderful wine
And sing till my heart doth break !

AMONG THE ACRES OF THE WOOD.

I.

I KNOW, I know,
  The way doth go
Athwart a greenwood glade, oh!
White bloom the wild-plums in that glade,
White as the bosom of the maid,
Who, stooping, sits, and milks and sings
Among the dew-dashed clover-rings,
When fades the flush, the henna blush,
  Of evening's glow, an orange low,
  And all the winds are laid, oh!

II.

I wot, I wot:
  And is it not
Right o'er the viney hill?
Say! where the wild-grapes mat and make
Penthouses to each bramble-brake,
And dangle plumes of fragrant blooms?
Where leaking sunbeams string the glooms
With beryl beads? where sprinkled weeds
  Blue blossoms fill? and shrill, oh, shrill,
  Sings all night long one whippoorwill?

III.

I ween, I ween
The path is green
'Neath beechen boughs that let
Sly glances of the bashful sky
Gleam usward like a girlish eye :
At night one far and lambent star
Shines limpid, like a watching Lar,
'Mid branching buds a tangled bud .   .   .
Where in the acres of the wood
    Blow strips of wet, wild violet,
    And only we have trysting met.

NOONING.

I.

WEAK winds that make the water wink ;
    White clouds that sail from lands of Fable,
To white Utopias of vague brink,
Down gulfs of blue unfathomable :
    Their rolling shadows drifting
    O'er fields of forest, lifting
Wild peaks of purple range that loom and sink.

II.

Warm knolls whereon the Nooning dreams ;
In droning dells that bask in brightness,
Low-lulled with hymns of mountain-streams,
Far-foaming falls of windy whiteness ;
    Where, from the glooming hollow
    With cawing crows that follow,
The hunted hawk wings wearily and screams.

III.

Dry-buzzing heat and drought that thrills
With one harsh locust's lonesome whirring ;

No answering voice shouts on the hills,
Receding echoes far-recurring—
>As when the Dawning dimpled,
>With hazel twilight wimpled,
From dewy tops called o'er responding rills.

IV.

Wan with sweet summer hangs the deep,
Hot heaven with the high sun hearted—
A wide May-apple bloom asleep
With golden-pistled petals parted.—
>Now—could befall,—her pouting
>Cheeks anger-red,—from sprouting
Rock-mosses some white wildwood Dream might
leap.

THE LOG-BRIDGE.

I.

L AST month, where the old log-bridge is laid
       O'er the woodland brook, in the belts o' the
         shade,
To the right, to the left, pink-packed was made
       A gloaming glory of scented tangle
By the bramble roses there—that wade
High-heaped on the sides—when they bloomed to
         fade,
And, wilting, powdered the ruts, and swayed
       To the waters beneath loose loops of spangle ;
When the breeze that blew and the beam that rayed
       Were murmurous-soft with the bees a-wrangle.

II.

This month—'t is August—the lane that leads
To the bramble-bridge runs waste with weeds,
That bloom bright saffron, or satin seeds
       Of thistle-fleece blow at you.   Hazy
And starry the lane with the thousand bredes
Of the yellow daisy—like sweet-eyed creeds
Peacefully praying.—Now by you speeds
       A butterfly sumptuous with mottle and lazy.
A yellowish-red, where the blue-bird pleads,
       The sumach's tassel dips down to the daisy.

III.

All golden the spot in the noon's gold shine,
Where the yellow-bird sits with eyes of wine
And swings and whistles ; where, line on line,
    In coils of warmth the sunbeams nestle ;
Where cool by the pool (where the crawfish, fine
As a shadow's shadow, darts dim) to mine
The wet creek-clay with their peevish whine,
    Come mason-hornets ; and roll and wrestle
With balls of clay they carry and twine
    In hollow nests on the joists o' the trestle.

IV.

Where the horsemint shoots through the grasses,—
    high
On the root-thick rivage that roofs,—a dry,
Gray knob that bristles with pink, the sigh
    Of crickets is sharp 'neath the dead leaves'
    bosoms :
When the woods grow dusk you will hear the cry
Of a passing bird flit twittering by ;
And the frogs' grave antiphons rise and die :
    And here to drink steal the wild opossums,
While lithe on those roots two lizards lie,
    Brown-backed like the bark, or stir the
    blossoms,

AMONG THE KNOBS.

THERE is a place embanked with brush
Three wooded knobs beyond,
Lost in a valley where the lush
Wild eglantine blows blonde.

Where light the dogwoods earliest
Their torches of white fires,
And, bee-bewildered, east and west
The red haws build white spires.

The wan wild apples' flowery sprays
Blur through the misty gloom
A pensive pink ; and by lone ways
The close blackberries bloom.

I love the spot : a shallow brook
Slips from the forest, near
The cane-brake and the violet nook,
Its rustling depths so clear.

The minnows glimmer where they glide
Above its rocky bed—
A long, dear, boyhood's brook, not wide,
Which has its sparkling head

3

Among the rainy hills ; and drops
  By four low waterfalls—
Wild music of an hundred stops—
  Between the leafy walls,

Against the water-gate, that hangs
  A rude portcullis,—dull
With lichened moss,—whose clumsy fangs
  The cress makes beautiful.

The glass-green dragon-flies about
  The seeding grasses swim ;
The streaked wasps, worrying in and out,
  Dart fretfully and slim.

Here in the moon-gold moss, that glows
  Like jets of moonlight, dies
The weak anemone ; and blows
  A flower less blue than skies.

And, where in April tenderly
  The dewy primrose made
A thin, peculiar fragrance, we,
  In the pellucid shade,

Found wild-strawberries half-abud,
  In May long berries,—fresh,
And pallid pink as wood-bird blood,—
  Stained many a trailing mesh.

Once from that hill a farmhouse 'mid
  Deep orchards—cozy brown
In lilacs and old roses hid—
  With picket-fence looked down.

O'er ruins now the roses guard ;
  The plum and seckel-pear
And the apricot rot on the sward
  Their wasted ripeness there.

But when the huckleberries blow
  Their waxen bells I 'll tread
Those dear accustomed ways, that go
  Adown the orchard, led

To that avoided spot, which seems
  The haunt of vanished springs ;
Lost as the hills in drowsy dreams
  Of visionary things.

LATE OCTOBER.

BULGED from its cup the dark brown acorn falls,
  And by its gnarly saucer, in the stream's
Clear puddles, swells ; the spiky spruce-gum balls
  Rust maces of an ouphen host that dreams ;
Beneath the chestnut-tree the burry hulls
  Split, and pour purses from their pockets' seams.

Burst silver white, nods,—an exploded husk
  Of snowy, woolly smoke,—the milk-weed's puff
Along the orchard's fence ; where in the dusk
  And ashen weeds,—as some grim Satyr's rough
Red, breezy cheeks burn through his beard,—the
      brusque
  Crab-apples laugh, wind-tumbled from above.

And through the wasted leaves the crickets' clicks
  Run feeble as a sound of fairy cheers.
One bird sits in the sumach, flits and picks
  Its sour seeds.   Far in the woods one hears
The drop of walnuts.   Round the straw's tall ricks,
  With lifted horns, one sees the lowing steers.

Some slim, bud-bound Leimoniäd hath flocked
  The birds, to lead them where the Southern
      foams

Sing of forgetfulness.   Where once were rocked
  Unnumbered bees within unnumbered blooms,
One languid bee crawls in one bloom and, locked
  Therein, dreams of the summer's oozing combs.

Winds shake the maples, and all suddenly
  A storm of leafy stars and whispers leaks
Down like a Dryad's coming.   To her knee
  Wading, the Naiad haunts her brook that streaks
Through golden waifs.   Hark !   Pan for Helike
  Flutes in the forest, while he seeks and seeks.

FALL.

FAR off a wind blew, and I heard
    Wide echoes of the woods reply—
The herald of some royal word
    From bannered trumpet blown to die
        On hills that held the sky.

The pomp of forests seemed to meet
    Bluff monarchs on a cloth of gold ;
Where berries of the bittersweet,
    That, splitting, show the coals they hold,
        Sowed garnets through the wold :

Where, under tents of maples, bredes
    Of smooth carnelians, oval red,
The spice-bush spangled : where, like beads,
    The dogwood's rounded rubies—fed
        With fire—blushed and bled.

To meet my dream my soul went out,
    And marked, 'mid richness cavalier,
A minne-singer—lips a-pout,
    A voice like music's—standing near,
        · A rose stuck in his ear :

Eyes, dancing like old German wine,
　All mirth and moonlight ; naught to spare
Of slender beard, that lends a line
　Unto his lip ; and, curling fair,
　　A chestnut wealth of hair.

His blue baretta's sweeping plume
　A beam of whiteness droops ; his hose,
Puffed at the thighs, of purple loom ;
　His tawny doublet, slashed with rose,
　　A dangling dagger shows :

A slim lute slants his breast.　.　.　I hear
　The leaf-crisp coming of his foot—
No wonder that the regnant Year
　Bends to his beauty, blushing mute,
　　And sighs to be his lute.

THE FOREST POOL.

ONE memory persuades me when
    Dusk's lonely star burns overhead,
To take the gray path through the glen—
    That finds the forest pool, made red
With sunset—and forget again,
    Forget that she is dead.

Once more to look long in the spring,
    That on one rock a finger white
Of foam that beckons still doth bring ;
    Some moon-wan spirit of the night
Who dwells among its murmuring,
    Her life the sad moonlight.

To see the red dusk touch it here
    With fire like a blade of blood ;
One star's reflection, white and clear
    As some wood-blossom's fallen bud ;
While all my grief stands very near,
    Pale in the solitude.

And it shall be before the moon
    Hangs—silver as a twisted horn

Blown out of elfland sweet with tune—
White in white clusters of the thorn,
That in the water, over soon,
    An image shall be born :

That has her throat of frost ; her lips,
    Her lips where God's anointment lies ;
Her eyes, wherefrom love's arrow-tips
    Break like the starlight of dark skies :
Her hair, a hazel heap that slips ;
    Her throat and hair and eyes.

And I shall stoop ; the water kissed,
    The face fades from me into air ;
Down in the wrinkled amethyst
    My own face sad as old despair ;
Then—night and mist ; and in the mist
    One dead leaf fallen there.

HAUNTED.

I.

WITHOUT a moon when night comes on
    There is a sighing in its trees
As of sad lips that no one sees ;
And the far-dwindling forest, large
Beyond fenced fields, seems shadowy drawn
Into its shadows.   Faint and wan,
By the wistariaed portico
Stealing, I go
Through gardens where the weeds are rank :
Where, here and there, in patch and bank,
Rise clumped the spiarees whose blooms
Seem dots of starlight ; and the four
Syringas sweet heap, powdered o'er,
Thin flower-beakers of perfumes ;
And the dead flowering almond-tree
Once maiden pink.   Still bower on bower,
The roses climb in blushing flower—
And from the roses shall I see
Her sad, sad eyes shine like the flowers,
That nestle dew-drops hours on hours,
Wistful, as if reproaching me ?

II.

When midnight comes it brings a moon :
A scent is strewn
Of honey and wild-thorns broadcast
Beneath the stars.   When I have passed
Under dark cedars, lonely pines,
To dodder-drowned petunias,
Corn-flower and pale columbine,
And mauve azaleas choked with grass,
White peonies like wisps of shine ;
Have passed by honey-suckle vines,
Piled deep and trammelled with the gourd
And morning-glory—one wild hoard
Of rich aroma—and have heard
The plaintive note of some lost bird
Trickle through night,—awakened where,
'Neath its thick lair of twisted twigs,
The jarring and incessant grigs
Hum,—dream-drugged so, the haunted air
Makes all my soul as heavy as
Dew-poppied grass.

III.

Once when the moon rose flushed and full,—
Like some sea-seen hesperian pool,
A splash of gold through tangling trees,—
There came slow sighings in the trees
As of sad lips that no one sees.
And when, all in a mystic space,

Her orb swam amiable white,
Right in yon shattered casement, by
The broken porch the creepers lace,
Made of a whisper and a sigh
I thought her face
Formed in a mist of tears ; so slight,
So beautiful, its pensive grace
Was like an olden melody.

IV.

I know, long-angled on its floors,
Where windows greet the anxious east,
The moonshine pours
White squares of glitter and, at least,
Gives glimmer to its moaning halls :
Sleep-tapestried, dim corridors
Wake whispers : by its wasted walls
Stand shadows : and where streaked dusts lay
Their undisturbed, deep gray,
Walk vision-footed sighs.   Below
I hear a murmur come and go
Through one great buckeye near her room.—
Ah ! know I not how those broad flues
Of her old home the winds make hoarse ?
Sonorous throats that growl and boom
With wafts that slink through avenues
Of summer, singing in their course,
Where blossoms drip, to swing them back ?

Its echoes, and the stealthy crack
Old, warping stairs give ; and the black
That drapes each room the mind informs
To fling from closets phantom arms ? . . .

V.

I see her face beseeching pressed
To the rugged, polished floor ; distressed,
Pinched in her blind and praying hands ;
So desolate with anguish, wrenched
With all remorse mind understands :
See him who stood and sneered and fled
Still unrelenting.   Then again
Myself come stealing in : fast-clenched
In staring eyes all the hard pain
Cramped to dilation, with a groan
To find a huddled heap alone—
Her white and dead.

VI.

Yes, there is moan
Of lamentation and hushed screams
In all its crannies and lean shades
Make melancholy rooms where braids
The lacy moonlight.   Slow have flown
The years ! the years ! and I have known
An anguish and remorse far worse
Than usual life's, and live, it seems,
Because to live is but a curse.   .   .   .

VII.

There lies the burying-place ; that ground
Gated with rusty iron ; stone
Squares in a mossy spot of dreams :
Wild just the same ; its roses waste
Limp, placid petals ; yonder some
Lie loose like puffs of foam
On bold, unhealthy weeds ; displaced,
Strew wiltings here my feet around.
Wild roses and wild thorns, where moan
The sorrowing wood-doves and
The sad days slumber bland.

GHOSTLY WEATHER.

WILD gusts of drizzle hoot and hiss
　　Through dodging lindens whistled through.
The dead's own days be days like this—
　　Yes, let me sit and be with you ;

Here in your willow chair whose seat
　　Spreads scarlet plush.　Hark ! how the gusts
In sad æolian cracks repeat
　　Mild moans !—They haunt your room, where
　　　　dusts

Make dim each ornament and chair ;
　　That locked-in memory where you died.
Since angels stood there, saintly fear
　　Guards each dark angle, mournful-eyed.

Through this dim day stoop your dim face ;
　　Gray eyes, like rain-drops, dimly deep ;
A soft gray cloudiness of lace,
　　Stand near me while I sleep, I sleep.

APOCALYPSE.

BEFORE I found you I had found
    Of your true eyes the open book
(Where re-created heaven wound
    Its wisdom with it) in the brook.

Ah, when I found you, looking in
    Those Scriptures of your eyes, above
All earth, o'ersoared earth's vulture, Sin,
    So apotheosized to love.

And, searching yet beneath it, saw
    The soul impatient of the sod—
What wonder then your love should draw
    Me to the nearer love of God.

UNCERTAINTY.

"'He cometh not,' she said."—MARIANA.

IT will not be to-day and yet
  I think and dream it will ; and let
The slow uncertainty devise
So many sweet excuses, met
By many sad, confuting lies.

The panes were sweated with the dawn ;
Yet through their dimness, shriveled drawn
The aigret of one princess-feather,
One monk's-hood tuft with oilets wan,
I glimpsed, dead in the slaying weather.

This morning when my window's chintz
I drew, how gray the day was !—Since
I saw him, yea, all days are gray !—
I gazed out on my dripping quince,
Defruited, gnarled, then turned away

To weep, and did not weep ; but felt
A colder anguish than did melt
About the tearful-visaged year :
Then flung the lattice wide and smelt
The autumn sorrow : Rotting near

4

The rain-soaked sunflowers, burnt and bleached,
Up which the frost-nipped gourd-vines reached,
Or morning-glories, seeded o'er
With ashen aiglets, whence beseeched
One blue bloom's brilliant palampore.

The podded hollyhocks—vague, tall,
Wind-battered sentries—by the wall
Rustled their tatters ; dripped and dripped
The fog thick on them.   Dying, all
The tarnished, hag-like zinnias tipped.

I felt the death and loved it : yea,
To have it nearer, sought the gray,
Chill, fading garth.   Yet could not weep ;
But only sigh some " well-a-way "
And yearn with weariness to sleep.

Mine were the fog, the frosty stalks,
The weak lights on the leafy walks,
The shadows shivering with the cold ;
The torpid cricket's dreary talks,
The last, dim, ruined marigold.

But when to-night the moon swings low—
A great marsh-marigold of glow—
And all my garden with the sea
Moans, then through phantom mist, I know
His shadow 'll come to comfort me.

OVERSEAS.

Non numero horas, nisi serenas.

WHEN fall fills morns with mist, it seems,
 In soul I am a part of it ;
Lib'rating on the humid beams,
 A form of frost, I float and flit
  From dreams to dreams. . . .

An old château sleeps 'mid the hills
 Of France : an avenue of sorbs
Conceals it : drifts of daffodils
 Bloom by a 'scutcheoned gate with barbs
  Like iron bills.

I pass the gate unquestioned, yet
 I feel announced. Broad holm-oaks make
Dark pools of restless violet.
 Between the bramble banks a lake—
  As in a net

The tangled scales twist silver—shines.
 Gray, mossy turrets swell above
The whispering leaves. Among the vines
 Rise ivied walls. A spot for love
  Beneath the pines.

Its angular windows, dimly seen
 From distant lanes with hawthorn hedged,
Beam broadly on the nectarine

Espaliered, and the peach-tree, wedged
    'Twixt climbing green.

Cool-babbling a fountain falls
    From gryphons' mouths in porphyry ;
Its carp swim eddying ; white balls
    Of lilies dip it when the bee
        Crawls in and drawls.

And butterflies, each with a face
    Of Faery on its wings, recline—
Beheaded pansies blown, that chase
    Each other—down the shade and shine
        Boughs interlace.

And roses ! roses, soft as vair,
    'Round sylvan statues and one old
Stone dial—Pompadours that wear
    Their royalty of purple and gold
        With saucy air.

Her scarf, her lute, whose ribbons breathe
    The perfume of her touch ; her gloves,
Modeling the daintiness they sheathe ;
    Her fan, a Watteau, gay with loves,
        Lie there beneath

A bank of eglantines that heaps
    A rose-strewn shadow. Naïve-eyed,
With lips as suave as they, she sleeps ;
    The romance by her, open wide,
        O'er which she weeps.

ACT III.

UPLIFTED darkness and the owl-light breaks,
    Scuds the wild land, pursuing patch with
        patch,
As when deep camomile a swift wind shakes.
How clumsily I raised the crazy latch !   .   .   .
So.—When yon black bulk, light-absorbing, rakes
Again the moon's bald disk—
Out ! and the storm may snatch
Again wet hair, pulled lank with wind and rain
Two hours since.—There from the ragged plain
A dark cloud-besom sweeps the beams again . . .
On ! on ! . . . What fear or risk ? . . .

Close to the fellside hugs the bramble hollow
Whining with wind, a pausing wind that grieves
Through the one crippled ash, whose nervous
        leaves
Worry and mutter, wooden as the lips
Of dead men kissing. There a gnarled vine slips
Up a humped, cloven rock, that seems to wallow
A gorgon head of ugly writhings ; heaves
When, heaped abruptly on it, *flare !*
Burst rain and tempest-glare.—
This passed, I follow

A thorny slip of path until
I reach the storm-scarred hill.

Shall I not then be breathless, sinking sense,
For ghastlier yet to come ?—Some sterner strength
Sustain my soul !—Beyond the hill the dense,
Dead wood remains and then . . . that livid
    length
Of mooning water, spectral and immense
With sullen storm and night . . .
There, if the ghoulish wind,—
Which knows well as I know how I have sinned,
—Will cease to curse me in its hag-like spite,
Disturbed with horror only of my soul,
I 'll see among cramped reeds, the storm has
    thinned,
His wide, white eyes, metallic in the light
Of the impassive moon ; in gusty roll
Of washing ripples, webby, slippery locks
Dabbling and dark. Or, wedged among fierce
    rocks,
Wild-pinched and water-strangled white,
His murdered face that mocks.

LOST LOVE.

I LOVED her madly. For—so wrought
  Young Love, divining Isles of Truth
  Large in the central Seas of Youth—
" Love will be loved," I thought.

Once when I brought a rare wild-pink
    To place among her plants, the wise,
    Still guerdon of her speaking eyes
Said more than thanks, I think.

She loved another. Ah ! too well
    I have the story in my soul !—
    A weary tale the weary whole
Of how she loved and fell.

I loved her so ! . . . Remembering of
    My mad grief then, I wonder why
    It is such griefs grow gray and die
While lives still live and love ?

Strange, is it not ? For grief was dear
    To me as she once. A regret
    It is now ; just to make eyes wet
And lift a big sob here.

Yet, had she lived as dead in shame
    As now in death, Love would have used
    Pride's pitying pencil and abused
The memory of her name.

This makes me thank my God, who led
    My broken life in sunlight of
    This pure affection, that my love
Lives by her being dead.

ON A PORTRAIT.

I.

AT seventeen she grew between
  His gaze and some old-world romance :
A face,—seductive and serene
As all that old romance may mean,—
  With dark eyes waking from a trance.
      At seventeen.

II.

At twenty-one no song might run
  More sweetly than his longing leapt
To her,—whose loveliness begun
For him all song beneath the sun,—
  With eyes of brown where laughter slept.
      At twenty-one.

III.

At thirty-two no dreams would do !—
  He loved this daughter of the South,
Whose eyes of blue his fancy drew,
What time the battle bugles blew
  To dash him on the cannon's mouth.
      At thirty-two.

AFTER THE TOURNAMENT.

I.

A ND shall it be, when white thorns flake
    With blossoms all the budding brake,
The rustle of one lifting leaf
    Will whisper low?
And one be near thee as thy grief—
    And wilt thou know?

II.

Or shall it be, when blows and dies
The forest columbine, two eyes
    Will bloom against thine faint as frost?
        Thou, deep in dreams,
    Wilt hark what plaintive winds sigh, lost
        In life that seems.

III.

Or shall it be, where rocks slope, smooth
With water-wear, where vague lights sooth,
    One in an old lute will beseech
        Thy listening ears
    With Provence melodies, that reach
        The soul like tears? . . .

IV.

Yes, this will be—Loop thy white arm
Beneath my hair . . . so ; let thy warm
　Blue eyes gaze in mine for a space,
　　A little while ;
　Love, it will rest me ; and thy face—
　　Ah, let it smile.

V.

Now art thou thou.　Yet—let thy hair,
A golden fragrance, fall ; thy fair
　Full throat bend low ; thy kiss be hot
　　With joy, not dry
　With anguish.—Sweet my Evalott !
　　Now let me die.

ORIENTAL ROMANCE.

I.

BEYOND lost seas of summer she
　　Dwelt on an island of the sea,
Last scion of that dynasty,
Queen of a race forgotten long.—
With lips of light and eyes of song,
From seaward groves of blowing lemon,
She called me in her native tongue,
Low-leaned on some rich robe of Yemen.

II.

I was a king.　Three moons we drove
Across green gulfs, the crimson clove
And cassia spiced, to claim her love.
Stuffed was my barque with gems and gold ;
Strips of rare sandalwood, grown old
With odor ; and pink pearls of Oman,
Than her chaste breasts less purely cold ;
And myrrh less fragrant than this woman.

III.

From Bassora I came.　We saw
Her condor castle on a claw

Of savage precipice, o'erawe
Besieging of the roaring spray :
Like some rough opal white it lay
Above us, all its towers a-taper,
Wherefrom, like an aroma, day
Struck splintered lights of sapphirine vapor.

IV.

Lamenting caverns dark, that keep
Sonorous echoes of the deep,
Moaned demon-haunted 'neath the steep. —
Fair as the moon whose light is shed
In Ramadan, the queen, who led
My love unto her island bowers,
I found . . . yea, lying young and dead
Among her maidens and her flowers.

PORPHYROGENITA.

I.

WAS it when Kriemhild was queen
　　That we rode by ways forgotten
Through the Rhineland, all serene
　　'Neath a low moon white as cotton?
I, a knight or troubadour?
Thou, a princess though a poor
　　Damsel of the Royal Closes?—
I have dreamed it somehow sure,
　　Reading of Kriemhilda's roses.

II.

Or in Venice by the sea
　　What romance grew up between us?
Thou a doge's daughter?—she
　　Titian painted as a Venus?
I, a gondolier whose barque
Glided past thy palace dark?—
　　Near Saint Mark's or Casa d'Oro?—
All thy casement sprang a-spark
　　At my barcarolle's " *Te oro.*"

III.

Klaia, one of Egypt; yea,
　　Languid as its sacred lily;

Didst with me a year and day
  Love upon the Isle of Philæ?
I, a priest of Isis?—Sweet,
'Neath the date-palms did we meet
  By a temple's pillared marble?
While from its star-still retreat
  Sank the nightingale's wild warble?

IV.

Have I dreamed that, I a slave,
  From thy lattice, O sultana!
Veilless, thy white hand did wave
  Me a Persian rose, sweet manna
Of thy lips' kiss in its heart?
That, through my Chaldæan art,
  With thy Khalif's bags of treasure,
From Damascus we did start
  Westward to some land of pleasure?

V.

Was it thou or, haply, thou?—
  Thou or thou, thou wast so dearest
That thy memory holds me now
  Like a passion; lying nearest
To dead evolutions of
Death to life and life to love:
  Truth invisible, but clearest
To the soul that looks above.

THE CASTLE OF LOVE.

He speaks.

I.

YOU ask how I knew that I knew it?—
    Like the king in the Asian tale,
I wandered on deserts that panted
With noon to a castle enchanted,
    That Afrits had built in a vale ;
    A vale where the sunlight lay pale
As moonlight.   And round it and through it
    I searched and I searched.   Like the tale

II.

No eunuch black-browed as a Marid
    Prevented me.   Silences seemed—
Nude slaves with the kohl and the henné
In eyes and on fingers—so many
    White whispers in dimness that dreamed
    Where censers of ambergris steamed :
And I came on a colonnade quarried
    From silvery marble, it seemed.

III,

And here a wide court rose estraded :
   Rich tulips, like carbuncles, bloomed
'Mid jonquil and jessamine glories ;
Strange birds, like the cockatoos, lories,
   Spread wings, like great blossoms, illumed,
   Or splashed in the fountain perfumed ;
Kept captive by network of braided,
   Spun gold where low galleries gloomed.

IV.

From nipples of five bending Peris
   Of gold that was auburn, in rays
The odorous fountain sprang calling :
I heard through the white water's falling,—
   More sweet than the laughter of sprays,
   Than songs of our happiest days,—
A music sigh soft, as if fairies
   Touched wind-harps whose chords were of rays.

V.

I searched through long corridors paneled
   With sandal ; whose doorways hung draped
With stuffs of Chosroës, deep-garded
With Indian gold : up the corded
   Stone stairway's bronze dragons that gaped ;
   Through moon-spangled hangings escaped—
5

'Twixt pillars of juniper channeled—
To a room constellated and draped.

VI.

As in legends :—of visions a vassal,
    One hears, yet beholds naught, and hears
A voice that encourages yearnings ;—
More subtle than aloes-wood burnings,
    The chamber sings, filled for the ears
    With melody ; nothing appears.—
My life found your soul such a castle,
    Your love is the music it hears.

CONSECRATION.

She speaks.

L AST night you told me, where we, parting,
    waited,
Of love somehow I 'd known before you told—
Long, long ago this love, perhaps, was fated,
    For why was it made suddenly so old ?

"Dear things we have and in their own truth
    cherish,
    Born with us seem, and as ourselves shall last ?
Part of our lives, we can not let them perish
    Out of our present's future or its past " ?

Then is it strange, dazed by that wider wonder,
    I, walking in the wood the morrow's dawn,
Should marvel not that, by my feet and under,
    The wildflowers now were purer than those gone ?

The wood-birds' silver warble sunk completer ?
    The sun shone whiter, lordlier at noon ?
And night, sweet God ! hung starrier, holier,
    sweeter,
    In Babylonian witchcraft of the moon ? .   .   .

All love hath emanations : an ideal
　Beats, beats within all beauty.　I was moved
No more when, dreamed, my spiritual dream rose
　　real,
　Than by what virtue, God divined, I loved.

ROMANTIC LOVE.

I.

IS it not sweet to know?—
The moon hath told me so—
That in some lost romance, love,
Long lost to us below,
A knight with casque and lance, love,
A thousand years ago,
I kissed you from a trance, love,—
The moon hath told me so.

II.

Or were it strange to wis?—
The stars have told me this—
Once sang a nightingale, love,
On some old isle of Greece ;
A wizard loved its wail, love,
That it might never cease,
From the full notes a woman,
More lovely than one human,
Devised . . . so goes the tale, love,—
The stars have told me this.

III.

Is it not quaint to tell?—
The flowers remember well—
Was once a rose that blew, love,
Pale in a haunted dell ;
And one, a Fairy true, love,
By loving broke the spell ;
And, lo ! the rose was—you, love !—
　　The flowers remember well.

IV.

To moon and flower and star
We are not what we are :
Sometimes, from o'er that sea, love,
Whose scolloped sands are far,—
From shores of Destiny, love,—
The winds that wing and war,
Will waft a thought that glistens
To Memory who listens,
Reminding thee and me, love,
　　We are not what we are.

PASTORAL LOVE.

THE pied pinks tilt in the wind that worries—
 Oh, the wind and the tan o' her cheek !
And the close sun sleeps on the rye nor hurries—
 And what shall a lover speak ?

The toad-flax flowers in flaxen hollows—
 Oh, the bloom and her yellow hair !
And the greenwood brook a wood-way follows—
 And what will his heart declare ?

The gray trees stoop where the daylight sprinkles—
 Hey, the day and the light o' her eye !
And a gray bird pipes and a wild fall tinkles—
 And what may a maid reply ?

Hey, the hills when the evening settles !
 Oh, the Edens within her eyes !
Say, the tryst 'mid the dropping petals !
 Lo, the low replies ! .   .   .

" Yes, when the west is a blur of roses "—
 " But   what   o'   the   buds   o'   thy   cheeks,   my
      dear ? "—
" Yes, when there 's rest and the twilight closes "—
 " And the star of love is near."

ANDALIA.

I.

SONG, that did waken you,
   Song that had taken you,
Has not forsaken you ;
   Still with the spring
My mad and merriest
Part of the veriest
Season and cheeriest :
   You, who can bring
Airs that the birds have taught you ;
Grace that the winds have brought you ;
Looks that the lilies laughed you ;
Thoughts that the high stars waft you—
   Are you a human thing ?

II.

Dreams—are you aught with them ?
You, who are fraught with them ;
You, like their thought, with them
   Beautiful too.
Life—you 're a gleam of it ;
Love—you 're a dream of it ;
Hope—you 're a beam of it,

Bound in the blue
Gray of big eyes that are often
Laughter and languor ; that soften
Over me sweetly and slowly
Out of your soul that is holy,
  And purer than dew.

III.

Face,—like the sweetest of
Perfumes,—completest of
Flowers God's fleetest of
  Months ever bear.
Sleep, who walk crisper, sleep,
Than the frost ; lisper sleep,
Have you a whisper, sleep,
  Soft as her hair?
Night and the stars did spin it ;
Stars and the night are in it—
Let but a ray of it bind me,
And, should the blind fates blind me,
  Fair I should know her, fair.

IV.

Love—has it mated you
One that awaited you,
One that was fated you
  Here for a while ?—
Song, can you sing in me

Sweeter, or bring in me
Peace, that will cling in me
So through all trial,
Such as her smiie ? like the morning's—
Fashioning luminous warnings,
Hints of a passion unspoken ;
Love, 't is your seal and its token !—
The light of her smile.

NOËRA.

N OËRA, when sad fall
Has grayed the fallow ;
Leaf-cramped the wood-brook's brawl
In pool and shallow ;
When sober wood-walks all
Strange shadows hallow :

Noëra, when gray gold
And golden gray
The crackling hollows fold
By every way,
Thee shall these eyes behold,
Dear bit of May ?

When webs are cribs for dew,
And gossamers,
Long streaks of silver-blue ;
When silence stirs
One dead leaf's rusting hue
Among the burs.

Noëra, in the wood
Or 'mid the grain,

Thou, with the hoiden mood
Of wind and rain
Fresh in thy sunny blood,
Sweetheart, again !

Noëra, when the corn
Reaped on the fields
The aster's stars adorn—
Their purple shields
Defying the forlorn
Decay fall wields :—

Noëra, haply then,
Thou being with me,
Each ruined greenwood glen
Will bud and be
Spring's with the spring again,
The spring in thee.

Thou of the breezy tread,
Feet of the breeze ;
Thou of the sunbeam head,
Heart like a bee's ;
Face like a woodland-bred
Anemone's.

So to October's death
An April part

Bring, while she taketh breath
Against death's dart ;
Noëra—one who hath
Made mine a heart.

Come with our golden year,
Come as its gold :
With thy same laughing, clear,
Loved voice of old :
In thy cool hair one dear
Wild marigold.

PHYLLIS.

I.

IF I were her lover
   I 'd wade through the clover
Over five fields or more ;
Over the meadows
To stand with the shadows,
The shadows that circle her door.
I 'd walk through the clover
    Close by her ;
And over and over
    I 'd sigh her,
" Your eyes are as brown
As a Night's looking down
 On waters that sleep
With the moon in their deep " . .
    If I were her lover to sigh her.

II.

If I were her lover
I 'd wade through the clover
Over five fields or more ;
And deep in the thickets
Or there by the pickets,

White pickets that fence in her door,
I 'd lean in the clover—
    The crisper
For the dews that are over—
    And whisper,
" Your lips are as rare
As the dewberries there,
Half ripe and as red,
On the honey-dew fed—"
    If I were her lover to whisper.

III.

If I were her lover
I 'd wade through the clover
Over five fields or more ;
And watch in the twinkle
Of stars that sprinkle
The paradise over her door.
And there in the clover
    I 'd reach her :
And over and over
    I 'd teach her,
A love without sighs,
Of laughterful eyes,
That reckoned each second
The pause of a kiss,
A kiss and . . . that is
    If I were her lover to teach her.

CARMEN.

LA GITANILLA ! tall dragoons
  In Andalusian afternoons,
With ogling eye and compliment
Smiled on you, as along you went
Some sleepy street of old Seville ;
Twirled with a military skill
Moustaches ; buttoned uniforms
Of Spanish yellow bowed your charms.

Proud, wicked head and hair blue-black,
Whence the mantilla, half thrown back,
Discovered shoulders and bold breast
Bohemian brown : and you were dressed—
In some short skirt of gypsy red
Of smuggled stuff : your stockings, dead
White silk, were worn with many a hole,
Through which your roguish ankles stole
Sly hints of plumpness : dainty toes
In red-morocco shoes with bows
Of scarlet ribbons.   Flirtingly
You walked by me, and I did see
Your oblique eyes, your sensuous lip,
That gnawed the rose, you once did flip

At bashful José's nose while loud
The gaunt guards laughed among the crowd.
And in your brazen chemise thrust,
Heaved with the swelling of your bust,
A bunch of white acacia blooms
Whiffed past my nostrils hot perfumes.

As in a cool *neveria*
I ate an ice with Mérimée,
Dark Carmencita, you passed gay
And holiday bedizenéd :
A new mantilla on your head ;
A crimson dress bespangled fierce ;
And crescent gold, hung in your ears,
Shone wrought Morisco ; and each shoe,
Of Cordovan leather, spangled blue,
Glanced merriment ; and from large arms
To well-turned ankles all your charms
Blew flutterings and glitterings
Of satin bands and beaded strings ;
Around each arm's tight thigh, one fold,
And graceful wrists, a twisted gold
Coiled serpents, jewelled in the head
With rubies of convulsive red.

In flowers and trimmings, to the jar
Of mandolin and gay guitar,
You, in the grated patio,
Danced : the curled coxcombs' staring row
6

Gave pleased applause. I saw you dance,
With wily motion and glad glance,
Voluptuous, the wild *romalis*,
Where every movement was a kiss
Of gracefulness, abandoned, wound
In your Basque tambourine's dull sound.
Or, as the ebon castanets
Clucked out dry time in unctuous jets,
Saw angry José through the grate
Glare on us a pale face of hate,
When some indecent colonel there
Presumed too lewdly for his ear.

Some still night in Seville : the street,
Candilejo : two shadows meet—
Flash sabres ; crossed within the moon,
Clash rapidly—a dead dragoon.

SEÑORITA.

A^N agate black, her roguish eyes
   Claim no proud lineage of the skies,
No velvet blue ; but of sweet earth
The reckless witchery and mirth.

Looped in her raven hair's repose,
A hot aroma, one tame rose
Dies ; envious of that beauty where—
By being near which—it is fair.

Two lyrics set to song, her ears ;
Whose unpretentious charm endears
The jewels whose harmonious fire
Binds the attention these inspire.

Two stars stop o'er her balcony,
Two eyes in heaven's canopy ;
No moon flows up the satin night
In pearl-pierced raiment spun of light.

From orange-orchards, dark in dew,
Vague, odorous lips the east-wind blew ;

Or she, a new Angelica
From Ariosto, breathed Cathay.

Oh, stoop to me ! and speaking reach
My soul like song, that learned low speech
From some sad instrument,—who knows ?—
Or flow'r, a dulcimer or rose.

AS IT IS.

M AN'S are the learnings of his books—
What is all knowledge that he knows
Beside the wit of winding brooks,
The wisdom of the summer rose !

How soil distils the scent in flowers
Baffles his science : heaven-dyed,
How, from the palette of His hours,
God gives them colors, hath defied.

What broad religion of the light,
Ere stars in heaven beat burning tunes,
Stains all the hollow edge of night
With glory as of molten moons.

Why sorrow is more strange than mirth,
And death than birth ; and afterward,
What sweetness in the bitter earth
Makes life's mortality so hard.

THOUGHTS.

I.

HOW the May-apple or
    Silvery cyclamen—
Star-perfect as a star—
    In woodland glade and glen
Blossoms, when breezes woo
With language of the dew,
Up to the broken blue
Of lonesome skies, do you
        Know or do I ?

II.

Can wild anemones
    Think ?—for they tremble so,
Pale with the mysteries
    Of the wind's joy and woe :
When the soft sunlight links
Crowns, where the dewdrop winks,
On every rose that shrinks,—
What its heart's aura thinks
        Know you or I ?   .   .   .

III.

Once when the Springtide trod
  By in a blowing blush,—
Wise as a gaze of God
  Holding all Heaven a-hush,—
Love was her thought ; and love
Through the vast soul above
Wrought so, these sprang thereof :
Thought into thoughts, to prove
  Symbols of love.

CHORDS.

I.

WHEN love delays, when love delays and joy
　　Steals, a strange shadow, o'er the happy
　　hills,
And hope smiles from to-morrow, nor fulfils
One promise of to-day, thy face would cloy
　　My soul with loved despair
　　By seeing thee so fair.

When love delays, when love delays and song
　　Aches at wild lips, regretful, as the sound
Of a whole sea strives in the shell-mouth bound;
Though hope smiles from to-morrow, all this wrong
　　Would, at one little word,
　　Leap forth for thee a sword.

When love delays, when love delays and sleep
　　Nests in dark eyeballs, like a song of home
Heard 'mid familiar flowers o'er the foam,
While hope smiles from to-morrow, thou wouldst
　　　steep
　　This hurt heart overmuch
　　In balm with one kind touch.

When love delays, when love delays and sorrow
  Drinks her own tears that fever her soul's thirst,
  And song, and sleep, and memory seem accurst,
While hope smiles from to-morrow, I would borrow
    One smile from thee to cheer
    The weary, weary year.

When love delays, when love delays and death
  Hath sealed dim lips and mocked young eyes
    with night,
  To love or hate locked calm, indifferent quite,—
Hope's star-eyed acolyte,—what kisses' breath.
    What joys can slay regret,
    Or teach thee to forget !

II.

If thou wouldst know the Beautiful that breathes
  Consanguined with the Earth, go seek !—but seek
No sighing shadows with dead hemlock-wreaths ;
  No sleepy sorrows whose wan eyes are weak
With vanished vigils, melancholy made,
Forlorn in lands of sin and saddening shade ;
No tearful angers torn of truthless love,
  That stab their own hearts to the dagger's hilt
For vengeance sweet ; no miser moods that fade
In owlet towers. Such it springs above,
  And buds on morning meads no flowers that wilt.

If thou dost seek the Beautiful, beware !
    Lest thou discover her, nor know 't is she ;
And she enslave thee evermore, and there
    Reward thee with the kingliest beggary :
Make thine the red rose of her cheek that stings ;
The kiss-sweet odor, thine, her wild breath brings ;
Make thine the broad bloom of her crownéd brow ;
    The prisoned lights that jewel her dark eyes ;
The melody—which is herself—that sings
The poem of her presence ; and the vow
    That gods exalts and mortals deifies.

Lone art thou then ; lone as the lone first star
    Kindling pale ardor o'er the dusk's gray wave ;
Lost to all happiness save searching far
    Through lands of life where death hath dug thy
        grave :
Lost—even as I—a devotee to her,
Poor in world-blessedness her bliss to share,
But rich in passion.—In her hermitage
    Hope no Arabian splendor, for it lies
Mossy by wooded waters ; hidden where
She, the pure priestess, wiser than what 's sage,
    'Shrines dreamers' hearts for godliest sacrifice.

III.

Now that the orchard's leaves are sear,
    And drip with rain instead of dew,

No moonbright fruit hangs moonlike here
And dead your long, white lilies too—
And dead the heart that broke for you.

How comes the dim touch of your arm ?
Your faint lips on my feverish cheek ?
Your eyes near mine ? deep as a charm,
And gray, so gray !—But I am weak,
Weak with wild tears and can not speak.

I am as one who walks with dreams ;
Sees as in youth his father's home ;
Hears from his native mountain streams
Far music of continual foam,
And one sweet voice that hails him home.

IMPRESSIONS.

1.

ON, towards the purlieus of impossible space,
From Death enamoured, Life capricious flies:
Communicated sorrow of his face
Freezing her ever backward burning eyes.

2.

Man's days are planted as a flower-bed
With labor's lily and the rose of folly :
Beneath grief's cypress, pale, uncomforted,
The phantom fungus blooms of melancholy.

3.

With starry gold Night still endorses what
Man's soul hath written, guessing at the skies :
Day on Night's scribble drops a fiery blot,
And thwart the writing scrawls " The lie of lies."

4.

And it may be that, seamed with iron scars,
One in vast Hell shall lift fierce eyes above,
And one, inviolate as God's high stars,
Gaze from sad Heaven, alas ! and see, and love.

5.

Into her heart's young crucible Life threw
Affliction first, then Faith,—by which is meant
Hope and Humility ;—Love touched the two,
And, lo ! the golden blessing of Content.

6.

As oft as Hope weighed coaxing on this arm,
On that Despair dashed heavily his fist :
He knew no way out of Grief's night and storm
Until a child called Effort came and kissed.

7.

Some obscene drug in her dull draught Sleep gave,
And, dead, I lived, to hear a man-faced beast
Dig, dig with wolfish fingers in my grave,
With horrible laughter to a horrible feast.

8.

Some few have pierced the phantom fogs, that veil
Life's stormy seas, into futurity,
And seen The Flying Dutchman's ominous sail,
Portentous of dark things that are to be :

Through hissing scud, mad mist, and roaring rain,
On thundering seas, they see her drive and drive,
Crowding wild canvas 'gainst the hurricane,
Her demon ports with battle-lamps alive.

9.

POETRY.

Who hath beheld the goddess face to face,
Blind with her beauty, all his days shall go
Climbing lone mountains towards her temple's place,
Weighed with song's sweet, inexorable woe.

10.

THE UNIMAGINATIVE.

Each form of beauty 's but the new disguise
Of thoughts more beautiful than forms can be :
Sceptics, who search with unanointed eyes,
Never the Earth's wild fairy-dance shall see.

11.

MUSIC.

God-born before the Sons of God, she hurled,
With awful symphonies of flood and fire,
God's name on rocking Chaos—world by world
Flamed as the universe rolled from her lyre.

12.

THE THREE ELEMENTS.

They come as couriers of Heaven : their feet
Sonorous-sandaled with majestic awe ;
With raiment of swift foam and wind and heat,
Blowing the trumpets of God's wrath and law.

13.

DESTINY.

Within the volume of the universe
With worlds she writes irrevocable laws :
From everlasting unto everlasting hers
The evolutions of effect and cause.

14.

FAME.

A mirror, brilliant as a beautiful star,
She lifts and sings to her own loveliness :
Not till her light and song have lured him far
Does man behold the lie he did not guess.

15.

THE HOURS.

With stars and dew and sunlight in your hair,
Approach, O daughters of the Day ! who saith,
" The gifts my children bring are Rest and Care,
Of which the last is Life, the first is Death."

16.

DESPAIR.

So sick at heart, so weary of the sun,
In her sad halls my Soul sits desolate,
Her Hope surrendered to Oblivion,
Whose coal-black charger neighs beneath the gate.

17.

THE MISANTHROPE.

Shut in with its own selfishness his soul
Sees—as a screech-owl in a hovel might,
Blinking avoided daylight through one hole—
The white world blackened by its own dull sight.

18.

ROME.

Above the Circus of the World she sat,
Beautiful and base, a harlot crowned with pride :
Fierce nations, upon whom she sneered and spat,—
Shrieked at her feet and for her pastime died.

19.

THE HUN.

On splendid infamies—a thousand years
Heaven tolerated—like a Word that trod
Incarnate of the Law, vast wrath and tears
In pagan eyes, behold ! the Scourge of God.

20.

GREECE.

The godlike sister of all lands she stands
Before the World, to whom she gave her heart,
Still testifying with degenerate hands
Her by-gone glory in enduring art.

21.

EGYPT.

With ages weighed as with the pyramids
And Karnac wrecks, still—out of Sphinx-like eyes
Beneath the apathetic lotus-lids—
With Memnon moan her granite heart defies.

22.

POE.

Night's raven o'er its portal and day's dove,
Wild witch-lights haunt an old-world-sculptured
    tomb :
Beside the corpse of beauty and of love
Song's everlasting-lamp burns in the gloom.

23.

HAWTHORNE.

Dim lands and dimmer walls, where magic slips
A couch of velvet sleep beneath romance :
Where speculation bends with longing lips
Fearful to break the long-unbroken trance.

24.

EMERSON.

Our New-World Chrysostom, whose golden tongue
Through nature preached philosophy and truth :
Wise intimate of loveliness he sung,
Old, yet instructing with the lips of youth.

7

25.

JAAFER THE VIZIER.

Lutes, odorous torches, slaves and dancing girls
In gardens by a moonlit waterside,
And one whose wise lips scatter gold and pearls—
Th' Arabian revels and the Barmecide.

26.

ON READING THE LIFE OF HAROUN ER RESHID.

Down all the lanterned Bagdad of our youth
He steals, with golden justice for the poor :
Within his palace—you shall know the truth—
A blood-smeared headsman hides behind each door.

FRAGMENTS.

I.

THE curtains of my couch sway heavily
　　Ere death divides the curtains of my soul.—
Sleep, like a gray expression of ghost lips
Heard through the moonlight of a haunted room,
Glides unto me, while death stands near and leers.

2.

" Stay not too long, love, stay not long away ! "
Said not my heart so when we kissed farewell ?
But now my heart is heavy with hard news
Of love that stooped for one last, bitter kiss.

3.

Tear from my heart and under furious feet
Trample the golden record of our love,
Love's golden language, O despair, despair !

4.

Night is a grave physician, who contrives
The drug of sleep to heal day's bruises up,

The drug of death for life's delirium.—
On lost expanses of a phantom land
Night stands : one hand of jewelled darkness points
Where, baleful beacons, burn two sinister stars,
Mournful o'er shadows of lugubrious hills
And lamentable tempest, and a shape
Placid and pale and silent utterly.

5.

O undivulging, unresponsive shape,
Is gold another name for power and crime?
Life, dust long dedicated unto death?
Death, darkness groping blindly towards a light?
Graven in gold do man's best deeds prevail,
Steadfast as tablets of the eternal stars?

IDEAL DIVINATION.

HOW I have thought of her,
  Her I have never seen !—
Now from a raying air
She, like a romance queen,
Flowers a face, serene,
Radiant in raven hair.

Now in a balsam scent
Laughs from the stars that gleam ;
Naked and redolent,
Bends to me breasts of beam,
Eyes that will make me dream,
Throat that the dimples dent.

Love is all vain to me
So : and as dust, severe
Faith : and a barren tree,
Truth : and a bitter tear,
Joy : for I wait and hear
Her who can never be.

Living, we learn to know
Life is not worth its pain ;
Living, we find a woe

Under each joy we gain ;
Fardled of hope we strain
Whither no hope may know.

Life is too credulous
Of time that beckons on.
Memory still serves us thus—
Gauging the coming dawn
By a day dead and gone,
Day that 's a part of us.

Soul—of life's sins so mocked,
Cloyed in the flesh and held,
Ever rebellion rocked,
Battling, forever quelled,
Yearning on heaven spelled
Over of stars—lies locked

Supine where torrents pour
Hellward ; on crags that high,
Scarred of the thunder, gore
Heaven ; the vulture's eye
Swims, and the harpies' cry
Clangs through the ocean's roar.

Notes of æolian light
Calling it hears *her* lips :
Scorched by her burning white
Arms and her armored hips,
Slimy each monster slips
Back to its native night.—

Rules she some brighter star ?
Inviolable queen
Of what the destinies are ?
She, with her light unseen
Leading my life, a sheen
Loftier than beauty far.

Oh ! in my dreams she lies
With me and fondles me ;
Amaranths are her eyes ;
And her hair, shadowy
Curlings of scent ; and she
Breathes at my heart and sighs.

If with its slaves I bear
All of life's tyranny,—
Worm for the worm,—I care
Naught if my spirit be
Hers in eternity—
Hers, who did make it dare.

THE BEAUTIFUL.

1.

OF moires of placid glitter
　The moon is knitter,
Under the jade-dark branches
The blue night blanches ;
Upon the torrent's arrow
Gleams flash, as narrow
As each blown tress of some pale sorceress,
Spell-haunted, slumbering in a wilderness.
　O soul, who dreamest, ponder :—
　Thy witch, thy love, what wonder
Of charms conceals her from thee powerless ?

2.

On mountain lakes of glimmer
White sheets of shimmer
Burn glassy, as if inner
Sea-castles,—thinner
Than peeled pearl-crystal curlings,—
Through eddy-whirlings
Sprayed glow of lucid battlement and spire,
The smoldering silver of their smothered fire :
　And hers, thy love's enchanted ?
　Where are her towers planted ?—
Heart ! that thou couldst besiege them with thy lyre !

3

By sands of ruffled beaches?
On terraced reaches
Of rolling roses, blowing
Mouths red as glowing
Cheeks of the folk of Fairy?
A palace airy,
With pointed casements, thrusts of piercing light,
Piled full of melody and marble-white?
Where beauty, veiled and hidden,
Smiles? who my life hath bidden
Come? by her wisdom accoladed knight?

4.

The blue night's sweetness settles—
Like hyacinth petals
Bowed by their weight of teary
Dew—dayward. Weary
One mocking-bird, moon-saddened,
Sings on; and gladdened,
My soul, dissolving, largens to the lie
Named Death by mortal lips.—Love, tell me why
I may not, thy defender,
Mix with thee? feel thy splendor
Expand me like a bud beneath God's eye?

SLEEP.

L OOK in my eyes !—Oh, the mild and mysterious
      Deeps of thine eyes that are holy with rest !—
Sigh to me ! yes, as thy cousin, imperious
Love, might, with lips that are soft and delirious,
      Soft with such pureness as blesses the blessed.
Fold all my soul in the mild and mysterious
           Might of thy rest.

All the night for thy love, all the night ! while the
           gladdening
      Presence of dusk as a legend of old
Speaks in me poesy : none of the saddening
Prose of the day that is sad with the maddening
      Heart of unrest that is heartless and cold.
All the night for thy love, all the night ! and its
           gladdening
           Beauty of old.

Scorn is not thine, nor is hate ; but the bubbling
      Fountains of strength that are youthful as morn's :
Hurt is not thine of remembrance ; the troubling
Bruises of waking whose fingers keep doubling—
      Doubling on temples life's cares that are thorns.
Thine are the hours of the stars and the bubbling
           Wells of the morns.

Pride and the passions of greed that now worry us,
  Mix with and brutalize ; envy and spite
At the heart, that 's an-ache with the tears that will
    hurry us
On, with the iron of anguish, to bury us,—
  Touch them and calm with thy fingers of white.
Make all these passions and pains, that now worry
    us,
        Night with the night.

Thine are the mansions of slumber ; the flowery
  Fields of the visions that blossom the dreams :
Thine, the high mountains of peace, that lie showery
Under the stars : and the valleys of bowery,
  Balmy forgettings made misty with streams :
Thine, the white halcyon mansions, the flowery
        Pastures of dreams.

Stay for me. Stand by me. Stoop to me. Pray
    for me.
  Pray, O thou essence, the incense of prayer !
Mother of hope ! whose kind eyes are a-ray for me,
Vestal with goodness, and fill all the day for me
  New with a vigor that masters despair.
Stay for me. Be of me breath of me. Pray for me,
        Sister of Prayer !

DISENCHANTMENT OF DEATH.

HUSH ! she is dead.   Tread gently as the light
    Steals in the weary room.   Thou shalt behold.
Look :—in death's ermine pomp of awful white,
    Pale passion of pulseless slumber, very cold,
Her beautiful youth !   Proud as heroic might—
    Death ! and how death hath made this vastly
      old.

Old earth she is now : energy of birth
    Hath fledged glad wings and tried them sud-
      denly ;
The eyes that held have freed their maiden mirth ;
    Their sparks of spirit, which made this to be,
Shine, fixed in rarer jewels not of Earth,
    In Fairylands beyond some silent sea.

A sod is this : whence, what were once those eyes,
    Will grow blue wild-flowers in what happy air !
Some weed with flossy blossoms will surprise,
    Haply, what summer with her affluent hair !
What roses bask those cheeks ! and the wise skies
    Will know her dryad to what young oak there !

The chastity of death hath touched her so,
   No dreams of life may reach her in her rest ;—
No dreams the heart exhausted here below,
   Sleep built within the romance of her breast.
How she will sleep ! like music, breathing slow
   Through the dark germs, to golden life caressed.

Low music, thin as winds that stir the grass,
   Smiting through red roots harpings ; and the sound
Of Elfin revels when the deep dews glass
   Globes of concentric beauty on the ground ;
For tepid clouds, through rainy nights that pass,
   The prayer in flowers that the stars have crowned.

So, if she 's dead, believe she is not dead.
   Disturb her not ; she lies so lost in sleep.
Its narrow house of care the soul hath fled.
   Her presence leans above us, and the deep
Is yet unvoyaged ; and the hand, that led
   Her meek feet forward, stays her shouldst thou
      weep.

To principles of passion and of pride,
   To trophied circumstance and specious law,
Stale saws of life, with scorn now flung aside,
   From Mercy's throne and Truth's, wouldst thou
      withdraw
Her, Hope in Hope, and Chastity's meek bride,
   In holiest Love of holy, without flaw ?

The anguish of the living,—merciless
   And bitter cruelty unto the grave,—
Wrings the dear dead with more than grief's dis-
   tress,
   Earth chaining love, bound by the lips that rave.
If thou hast sorrow, let thy sorrow bless
   The conqueror who leaves us less a slave.

" Unjust "?—He is not.   Yea, hast thou not all,
   All that thou ever hadst when this dull clay,
Thy long belovéd, made the spiritual
   A restless vassal of Earth's night and day?
This hath been thine and is : the cosmic call
   Hath but reclaimed its own and borne away.

Thou unjust !—Bar not from its high estate,—
   Won with what toil through devastating cares !
What bootless battling with the violent Fate !
   What mailed endeavor with resistless years !—
The soul, Heaven granted thee as earthly mate ;
   Being only loaned, return it not with tears !

THE THREE URGANDAS.

I.

CAST on sleep there came to me
Three Urgandas from the sea
Moaning out of Briogne :
Cloudy-clad in awful white ;
And each face, a lucid light,
Rayed and blossomed out of night.

2.

In my sleep I saw them rest,
Each a long hand at her breast,
Like the half-moon in the west :
Hair, like hoarded ingots, rolled
Down their shoulders, burning cold,
An insufferable gold.

3.

Rosy round each high brow bent
Fourfold starry gold that sent
Barbs of fire redolent :
'Neath their burning crowns their eyes
Shone like stormy stars the skies
Rock in shattered storm that flies.

4.

Wisdom's eyes of lurid dark ;
And each red mouth, like a spark,
Flashed and laughed off care and cark :
Mouths for song and lips to kiss ;
Lips for hate and mouths to hiss ;
Mouths that fashioned pain or bliss.

5.

Tall as stately virgins dead,
Tapers lit at feet and head,
Round whom Latin prayers are said :
Or as vampire women who,
Buried beauties, rise and woo
Youths whose blood they suck like dew.—

6.

And the west one said to me :
" Thou hast slept thus holily
While seven sands ran secretly.
Earth hath served thee like a slave,
Serving us who found thee brave,
Faithful in the life we gave :

7.

" Know ! "—She touched my brow ; a pain
As of arrows pierced my brain ;
Ceased ; and earth fell, some vast strain—

And I understood all thought ;
What life is, the spirit fraught ;
Love and hate ; how worlds are wrought.

8.

And the east one said to me :
" Thou hast wandered wearily
By what mist-enveloped sea !
Know the things thou hast not seen :
Life and law, and love and teen ;
Things that be and have not been :

9.

" See !"—Her voice sobbed like a lyre,
Comprehending all desire
In its gamut's singing fire—
Lifting inner eyelids, which
Dimmed clairvoyance, with a twitch,
All my soul with light was rich :

10.

And I saw the eyes of sleep ;
Nerves of change that rule the deep ;
Laws of entity that sweep
Orbs and eons ; springs of power ;
Circumstance, blown like a flower ;
Time, the fragment of an hour.—

8

11.

'Neath the central third one's will,
Balanced being that did thrill,
All my soul lay very still,
As she sternly stooped to me :—
" Thou dost know, and thou canst see ;
What thou art arise and be ! "

12.

To my mouth her lips she pressed ;
And my naked soul, thrice blessed,
Quaffed her radiance and caressed ;
Mounted and vibrating fled ;
Soared with her to them that said,
" Thou dost live and thou art dead."

THE LEGACY OF DEATH.

THE moonbeams on the hollies glow
   Pale where she left me ; and the snow
Lies bleak as moonshine on the graves,
Ribbed with each gust that shakes and waves
Ancestral cedars by her tomb. . . .

She lay so beautiful in death,
In death's dim loveliness, the gloom,
The iciness that takes the breath,
The sense of worms, were not too strong
To keep me from beholding long.

I stole into the mystery of
Her old, armorial tomb ; and love
Sighed all its romance to my heart.
Soft indistinctness of pale lips
Breathed on my hair ; faint finger-tips
Fluttered their starlight on my brow ;
Vague kisses touched my eyes, and now,
Hard on my lips, an aching sense
Of vampire winning. And I heard
Her name slow-syllabled—a word
Of haunting harmony—and then
Low-whispered, " Thou ! at last, 'tis thou ! "
And sighs of shadowy lips again.

How madly strange that this should be !
For, had she loved me when of earth,
It were not now so marvellous,
So marvellous, remembering me
With dead for living love, though worth
Less, yes, far less to both of us.
And so I wondered, listening there,
" What deed of mine, or thought hath wrought
This love from hate in after-life
She giveth back ?" and everywhere
Around my life I thought and thought
And—nothing ; only, how my love
Had still persisted 'neath her hate
That made her Appolonio's wife.
Her hate ! her lovely hate !—for of
Her naught I found unlovely—and
I felt she did not understand
My passion, so 't were well to wait.

And now I felt her presence near,
I full of life, yet had no fear
There in the sombre silence, mark.
And it was dark, yes, deadly dark ;
But when I slowly drew away
The pall, death modeled with her face,—
From face and limbs it fell and lay
Rich in the dust,—the shrouded place
Was glittering daggered by the spark
Of one wild ruby at her throat,
Red-arrowed with star-heated throbs

That made it pulse. And note on note
The darkness fought with tenuous sobs
Of glimmering from out that stone,
Lustrous and large against her throat
As her large eyes when they could see ;
And standing by the dead alone
I wondered not that this should be.

Red essence of an hundred stars
In fretful crimson through and through
Its bezels beat, when, bending down
My hot lips kissed her mouth. And scars
Of veiny scarlet and of blue,
Flame-hearted, blurred the midnight, and
The vault rang—and I felt a hand
Like fire in mine. And, lo, a frown
Broke up her face as gently as
A breeze that jolts the ripening grass
And spills its rain-drops. When this passed,
Through song-soft slumber binding fast,
Slow smiles dreamed outward beautiful ;
And with each smile I heard the dull
Deep music of her heart and saw,
As by some necromantic law,
Faint tremblings of a lubric light
Float through white temples and white throat ;
And each long pulse was as a note,
That gathering, like a strong surprise
With all its happiness, again
Left her arch lips one wistful smile

That lingered languidly : yet pain
Ached 'neath her eyelids, making sight
Insufferable. . . . Yet those eyes
Grew wide unto my kisses—yea,
They were unsealed ! And all the fire
Of that dark ruby at her throat,
Arrow by arrow, into them smote ;
And as some harmony entire
Was she, but how, I can not say.

And forth into the night I brought
Her beautiful ; and o'er the snow
Where moonbeams on the hollies glow,
I led her. But her feet no print,
No lightest trace in frost, no dint
Left of their nakedness. I thought,
" The moonlight fills them with its glow
And covers ;—and the tomb was black,
Then this strong light—yes ! " turning back
My eyes met hers ; and as I turned,
Flashing centupled facets, burned
That red gem at her throat ; and I
Studied its beauty for a while :
" How came it there, and when, and why ?
Who set it at her throat ? again,
Why was it there ? " So pondering
I questioned. And a far, strange smile
Filled all her face, and secret pain
Gave to her words a bitter ring :
" Thou ! thou ! alas ! " she said and sighed ;

" And if I am not dead, 't is thou !
See where thy heart's-blood beateth now,
Here ! " and she leaned unto me, eyed
Like some wise serpent that hath still
Lain all night on wild rocks to stare
At labyrinthine stars until
Its eyes have learned their golden glare.

And then I took her by the wrists
And drew her to me. Faintly felt
The sorrow of her hair ; whose mists
Fell twilight-deep and dimly smelt
Still of the shroud and tomb. And she
Smiled on me with such sorcery
As well might win a soul from God
To fiends and furies. And I trod
On white enchantments and was long
A song and harp-string to a song,
Love's battle in my blood. And there
Kissing her throat, her mouth, her hair,
I stole the jewel from her throat
With crafty fingers, to admire
The witchcraft of its fevered fire :
It, in the hollow of my hand,
A rosy spasm seemed to float,
A heart of anger fiercely fanned
With red convulsions : like a brand
I felt it scorch me ; felt it run
Swift through my pulses like a sun
Of torrid poison. And I marked

My palm brim full with blood ; and slow
Big drops drip beads of oozing glow,
Like holly-berries, on the snow.

Then all the night, contracting, darked
Upon me and I heard a sigh
So like a moan, 't was as if years
Of anguish bore it : and the sky
Swam near me as when seen through tears :
And she was gone. .   .   .   In ghostly gloom
Of dark, scarred pines a crumbling tomb
Loomed like a mist.   Carved in its stone
Above the lintel, dim and deep,
Glimmered the legend of her sleep :
" *Love crowned with death our lovely one.*
Our hearts bow by her side and weep.
And one sits weeping all alone."

I.

THE CAVERNS OF KAF.

[*Love Sensual.*]

" ' *Where am I?* ' *cried he ; ' what are these dreadful rocks ? these valleys of darkness ? are we arrived at the horrible Kaf ? ' "*—VATHEK.

ONE Benreddin, I have heard,
  Near the town of Mosul sleeping,
In a dream beheld a bird,
  Wonderful with plumes of sweeping
Whiteness crowned pomegranate-red :
Ever near him still it fled
Brilliant as a blossom : keeping
Near the Tigris, him it led.

Following, Benreddin came
  To a haggard valley, shouldered
Under peaks that had no name :
  Here it vanished : on the bouldered
Savageness a woman, fair
In a white simarre, rose there,
Auburn-haired : around her smouldered
Pensive lights of purple air.

And she led him down to vast
   Caves of sardonyx, each ceiling
Domed with chrysoberyl : blast
   In blast of music,—stealing
Out of aural glories,—nears ;
Rushing on his eager ears
To recede in echoes, pealing
Psalteries and dulcimers.

Wildly sculptured slabs did weave
   Walls of story ; where, embattled,
Warred Amshaspand and the Deev ;
   Over all two splendors rattled
Arms of Heaven, arms of Hell ;
Forms of flame that seemed to swell
Godlike : Aherman who battled
With Ormuzd he shall not quell.

And Benreddin wondered till
   The reverberant music drifting
Strong beyond his utmost will,
   Rolled him onward where, high lifting
Pillar and entablature,
Vast with emblem, yawned a door—
Valves of liquid lightning shifting
In and out and up and o'er.   .   .   .

Walls of serpentine deep-domed
   Green with agate and with beryl ;
Tortuous diaper crusted foamed
   Rough with jewels : and, as peril

Difficult, a colonnade
Ran of satin-spar to fade
Far in labyrinths of sterile
Tiger-eye that, twisting, rayed.

Dizzy stones of magic price
   Crammed volute and loaded corbel ;
Iridescent shafts of ice
   Leapt : with long reëchoed warble
Waters unto waters sang :
Curling arc and column sprang
Into fire as each marble
Fountain flung its drift that rang.

And around him, filled with sound,
   Surfs of resonant colors jetted :
Sun-circumferences that wound
   Out of arcades, crescent-fretted,
Mists of citron and of roon,
Lemon lights that mocked the moon,
Shot with scarlet, veined and netted,
Beating golden hearts of tune.

Discs of rose and lily-hue :
   Orbs of down-dilating splendor ;
In whose centers slowly grew
   Spots like serpent eyes that, slender,
Glared with undecided beams ;
Burning through dissolving gleams,
Hissed a trail of fire, tender
As an houri's breath who dreams.

Characters of Arabic,
   Cabalistic, red as coral,
Through vague violet veils flashed quick,
   Changing ; as if fierce at quarrel
Iran wrote of Turan there
Hate and scorn, or everywhere
Wrought swift talisman and moral
Stern the Afrits dare not dare.

Sounding splendors led him on
   To a crystal cavern ; hollow
Hewn of alabaster wan,
   Lucid, whence his gaze could follow
Far transparent flights in flights
Rolling ; drowned in singing lights
Glaucous gold ; he like a swallow
O'er a lake the morning smites.

Down the dome laughed out and in
   Sensuous faces of the Peris :
Restless eyes of Deevs and Jinn
   In the walls watched : unseen faeries
Out of rainbows rained and tossed
Flowers of fire full of frost ;
Blossoms where the fire varies
And the smouldering scent is lost.

Still below these, face to face,
   Seven odalisques of Heaven
Swung within a silver space
   Flaming censers ; and the seven

Crowned with stars of burning green,
Mounted cloudy incense, seen,
As it rose, to be a driven
Hippogrif or rosmarine :

Aloes, Nard and Ambergris,
  Sandal, Frankincense and Civet,—
Riders of the fragrances,—
  Rein each wild aroma ; give it
Spurs and race it down the lull
Of the caverns, clouded dull
With white steeds of musk they rivet
Vaporous and beautiful.

And Benreddin's passive soul,
  To hot eyes intoxicated,
Ached ; and, drinking at the whole
  Fountain of fierce Passion, sated
Drank unsatisfied.   It saw
Cheeks of light without a flaw,
Breasts of bloom with breathings bated,
Limbs translucent nearer draw.

Houri eyes and wafted hair
  Brilliant blackness.   Then a thunder
Of hoarse music, that did bear
  Upward, organed in the under
Caverns of the demon world.
Koran scrolls of glisten curled
Sparkling by him ; and a wonder
Of cœrulean mottoes swirled.

Then one long note made of sighs.—
　A muezzin cry repeated,
Dying downward.—Burning eyes,
　Melting from him, passion-heated.
Then sad voices, far away,
Choral.　Then one rocking ray
Angry flamed and angry fleeted
From a violent red to gray.

And, 't is told, this one was young,
　Young that morning.　When the darting,
Anguish-throated bulbuls sung,
　Through the silent starlight starting,
One, a Baghdad merchant, led
By the white light on its head,
Found a hoary shadow.　Parting
Hair from face, Benreddin—dead.

II.

THE SPIRIT OF THE VAN.

[Love Ideal.]

"*Among the mountains of Carmarthen, lies a beautiful and romantic piece of water, named The Van Pools. Tradition relates, that after midnight, on New Year's Eve, there appears on this lake a being named The Spirit of the Van. She is dressed in a white robe, bound by a golden girdle; her hair is long and golden, her face is pale and melancholy.*"—FAIRY MYTHOLOGY.

MIDSUMMER-NIGHT; the Van; through
    night's wan noon,
Wading the storm-scud of an eve of storm,
Pale o'er Carmarthen's peaks the mounting moon.—
Wilds of Carmarthen ! sullen heights that swarm
Girdling lone waters—as gaunt wizards might
    Crouch guarding some enchanted gem of charm—
Wilds of Carmarthen, that for me each night
    Reëcho prayers and pleadings,—all the year
Unanswered, made to listening waters,—white,
    The bitter white of Winter, and the clear

Cool eyes of girlish Springtide, and the slow
   Sweet gaze of languid Summer, and the dear
Dark eyes of tristful Autumn saw me so,
   Unhappy, lost among your moaning hills !

Should any ripple tremble into glow,
   When yeasty moonshine scuds the foam, there
     thrills
Heart's expectation through glad veins and high
   With " She ! " each pulse the exultation fills.
But she 't is never.   Once . . . and then would I
   Had fall'n abolished so beholding ! . . . World,
What sadder hast than beauty that must die ?—
   Once I beheld her !—if some fiend had curled
Stiff talons through my hair, and, twisting tight,
   Scoffed, " Burn and be !" then into hell had hurled
Me satisfied with beauty—beauty's white
   Bloom heavenizing hell—I, unamerced,
Shackled with tortures, might have mocked hell's
     spite.

Immortal memory of love, I thirst !
O starlike beauty that the memory wove,
   In that I love thee am I so accursed ?—
Oh, make me mad with love, with all thy love !
   Who tell it to these wilds when midnights gloom
Storms or drip gold from sibylline stars above :
   Let thy high favor all heaven's fires consume !
Quench with thy starry presence ! and make mad
   Me with sweet madness ! slay me with perfume !

Sleep may I not now for all sleep is sad.
  Cheated of thee, sad are all tearful dreams
A shadowy sorrow haunts with what hath clad
  Day's tyrannous hope in life that only seems :
And seeming hope forever needs must pine
  Seeking evasions that are form-fixed gleams.—
Though thou be wrought from elements divine,
  And I crass earth exalted, which will think,
" Since I am thine this makes me think thee
    mine,"
Must I, its usual phantom, the still brink
Of thy lone lake bewilder nightly ? Yearn
  For that bright vision of a moment's wink ?
When, glassing out great circles, which did urn
  Some intense essence of interior light,—
As clouds, that clothe the moon, unbinding burn,
  Riven, erupt her orb, triumphant white,—
Middle the Van foam, churned to feathering fire,
  Dilated ivory-wan. Expectant night
Tip-toed attentive, fearful to suspire,
  When there uprose—what pure divinity ?
What goddess sensed with glory and desire ?
  One melancholy instant born to be—
Love's ! and sunk back where burst a brassy
    black
  O'er glittering waves that sighed with ecstasy.—
Thou ! in whose path harmonious hues bloomed
    back,
  Pale pearl and lilac, asphodel and rose,
Like many flowers blooming in thy track.
  9

And I alone ; to marvel as who knows
He is not dead and yet it seems he is,
　　Tranced but in body while the spirit glows.—
O world-sweet face ! brow one white, angel kiss !
　　High immortality !—To fancy such,
Dance starlight in a lily's loveliness.—
　　Waist-bound with moony gold, too base to clutch
Her godlike chastity, though clear as gum
　　That almugs sweat, and fragrance to the touch !
And hair—not hair ! gold rays, like those that come
　　Strained through the bubble of a chrysolite,
Curled quiverings of light that clung and clomb.
　　Such left me such ; deep on my soul's quick sight
Eternal seared ; my life—a stealing shade
　　Avoiding day and ardent for the night :
A raver to the hoary hills which laid
　　Their dumb society in ruth on who
Shunned all companionship of man and maid :
　　Boon comrade of the mountain blossoms blue :
Instructed intimate of trees, that they—
　　Wise as the legendary world that drew
Oracles from lips in oaks—might haply say
　　Prophetic precepts to him : how were won
A spirit loved to love a mortal.—Yea,
　　In vain !

　　Yet one day, log-like in the sun
Beside a cave,—the mandrake vines made rank,
　　And hairy henbane, where huge spiders spun,—
Wrinkled as Magic, I a grizzled, lank,

Squat something startled ; naught but skin and
 hair,
With eyes wherein two demons brewed and drank
 Disputing dreams, which made them shrink or
  glare ;
Familiars that,—beholding me draw near,—
 With frog-like lips croak'd at me, " Do and
  dare !
Woo her with thy heart's actions ; making clear
 Thy soul's white passage for her coming feet.
Climb to her love and crawl ! Fear naught but
 fear ! "

Thus have I done these many months. Repeat
Acts of the heart with passionate offering
 Of love whose anguish makes it seven-times
  sweet.
Still all in vain, in vain. Now I but bring
 My simple self to-night, unfearing, see !
Myself unto thee !—Shall this clay still cling
 Clogging fulfillment ? thy love's mastery
Be balked by flesh ? No ! let me plunge and fly
 Deep to thy mounted throne of majesty !
Gaze in thine eyes one splendid instant—die
 To epochs of the elements ! One kiss
Of thine to give me immortality !
 Part of thy breathing waves, that laugh and hiss
With tides,—thy winds,—that rock the awful
 deeps,
 Or build with song vast temples for thy bliss :

To thrill responsive as thy white hand sweeps
  The chords of some sad shell, and dream and
    roam
Through glaucous chambers where the green day
    sleeps !
  Dead not with death !—

                        What secrets hath thy home
Not mine then, storied in exultant foam ?—
Deeper, down deeper ! yea, behold, I come !

III.

THE SPIRIT OF THE STAR.

[Love spiritual.]

" *This union of the human soul with the divine æthereal substance of the universe, is the ancient doctrine of Pythagoras and Plato : but it seems to exclude any personal or conscious immortality.*"—DIVINE LEGATION.

THERE is love for love : the heaven
    Teems with possibilities :
Earth hath such as heaven hath given
    Earth and all her sister seas.
Heaven and earth and sea is gladder
For it ; only man is sadder,
Waxing wise in night for driven
    Drift of light he never sees.

There are lives for lives ; and beauty
    Born for beauty on the earth ;
Faith for faith's immortal booty
    Ris'n to some celestial worth :

Song for every song ; unfolding
Hope for dying hope ; a holding
Duty towards aspiring duty,
  Godly as the laws of birth.

Earth and ocean are prolific
  Of God's wonders as our sky ;
With wild shapes of fair, terrific,
  Who, if loved, shall never die :
Dæmons rugged as their mountains ;
Spirits sunny as their fountains ;
Sylphids of the wind, pacific
  As the stars they tremble by . . .

I was lonely ; long had waited
  For the sweet, eternal sleep ;
Watching where the worlds dilated,
  Waned or wasted in the deep :
Where beneath my star a planet
Whirled and shone like glowing granite,
While around it ne'er abated
  Orbs of fire in their sweep.

I was sad ; the silence wilted
  Round me like a scentless bud
Fading ere it blows.   The quilted
  Clouds, like bursts of rushing blood
Streamed beneath me.   And the starry
Blue serene above arched, barry
With the golden stars, that filled it
  With their lofty sisterhood.

I was loveless with a yearning
   After love that never came ;
All my astral passion burning
   Outward ; to no blushing shame
Immolated ; but a splendor
Of intention that was tender
To compulsion ; all returning
   On my heart with fiercer flame.

So I left the stars whose lances
   Shook their arrowy gold in heat
Of hard hyacinth ; the glances
   Of their million moony feet
Ranged about me leaving. Beating
Downward, left them still repeating
Far farewells ; and through the trances
   Of dark space their eyes looked sweet.

Passed your moon : saw melancholy
   Alabaster summits sharp ;
Cataracts of crystal volley
   Over silver crag and scarp :
On the mountains,—like a story
Of high Heaven revealed in glory,—
Growing as if music slowly
   Built it, rolling from a harp,—

Rose a city : cloudy nacre
   Were its walls, that towered round
Acre upon arching acre
   Of a marble-terraced ground :

Caryatids alternated
With Atlantes sculpture-weighted ;
And its gates—some god the maker—
Valves of symboled diamond.

In the pure light glittered swimming
Domes of dazzle ; swirl on swirl,
Columned temples bubbled brimming
Roofs of daedal-emblemed curl ;
Galleries of moonstone darkled ;
Palaces, whose pillars sparkled
Misty opal ; and, far dimming,
Aqueducts of ghostly pearl.

I beheld it and descended
Earthward. For the longing drew
Me, and drawing me was blended
With a world I never knew.
And, did every star forsake me,
I had answered what did take me
Earthward, where it swung its splendid
Sphere along the rocking blue.

And when night came, lo, above you,
Sleeping by your folded sheep,
O'er the hills I rose. To love you
Came, and kissed you in your sleep.
And the destinies had wrought it
So you knew me. You, who thought it
Not so strange that I should love you,
I a spirit of the deep.

Ah, you knew how she had found you
  Sometime in some life not sad ;
Won your soul to hers and bound you
  With chaste kisses that were glad :—
Men forget, but we remember !—
And the love, that made an ember
Of your soul once, falls around you—
  And your nakedness is clad.

Being Beauty's now,—one petal
  Of its passion-flower,—far
Past Earth's ignorance—a metal,
  Rusted, that reflects no star—
Live beyond men lest they shame you !
Lest their shame, not I, should blame you !
Dream ! and when the shadows settle,
  Be the dream you dream you are !

LYANNA.

" *These elementary beings, we are told, were by their constitution more long-lived than man, but with this essential disadvantage, that at death they wholly ceased to exist. In the meantime they were inspired with an earnest desire for immortality; and there was one way left for them, by which this desire might be gratified. If they were so happy as to awaken in any of the initiated a passion the end of which was marriage, then the sylph became immortal.*"—LIVES OF THE NECROMANCERS.

THE Summer came over the southern ocean
    Girdled with fire, tiaraed with light ;
Laughter her eyes and her lips—a potion
    To quaff with kisses and know its might :
A shadow that sparkled and flashed ; a motion
    Blushed from the uttermost south, and I,
Of the race of the Sylphs, far over the ocean
    Followed her up the sky.

An exile I to the mists that cluster,
    Pulsing with pearl and braided with blue,
Large, luminous domes where the organs bluster
    Low of the winds ; where my brother-crew,

When the day dreams up, in their bright bands
    muster,
  Ranges of glitter through cloudy gold,
At the gates of the Dawn, whose limbs are lustre,
    To wait till her gates unfold.

For the Summer murmured me, " Follow ! follow !"
  Whispered, and promising whispered, " Love !"—
Winged with the wings of the sweeping swallow,
  I followed the wings of the drifting dove :
" Love, and a mortal," and fain did I follow ;
  " Love, and immortal," my flight was strong ;
" Life !" and my life seemed vain and hollow ;
    " Love ! " and my heart was song.

Fleet as the winds are fleet, yea, and fleeter
  Far than the stars, that throbbed like foam
Through the billowy blue, in musical meter
  Winnowed our wings ; and the golden gloam
Rang ; and life was a passion, completer
  Than Edens of flowers ; and faith, a lyre
That sang at the heart to make hope sweeter,
    And hope, a leaping fire.

So to the north our wings went maying
  Resonant ways, till a castle shone
Gaunt on great cliffs, and the late skies graying
  O'er walls of war and o'er towers of stone.

A fall of steps to the sea where, spraying,
　　Thundered the breakers ; and terrace and stair,
Rock o'er the waters, rose rosy and raying
　　　　Deep in the sunset glare.

A dewdrop burns when the dawn lights prickle :
　　All of my being tingled with light,
Blossomed against her tarrying, fickle
　　White on the terraced height :
Beauty that stood like a moon in sickle,—
　　A slender moon that the winds bleach bleak,
With its hue like honeys that drip and trickle
　　　　From combs whose wax is weak.—

In dreams I came to her, lo ! as a vision :
　　Yea, in her sleep as a dream was wound :
Of her vestal chastity held : a prison
　　Her innermost spirit that took and bound.
And her rest I stole ; for sleep in derision
　　Mocked at my hope for a love that slept :
So her soul I awakened ; lo ! it had risen,
　　　　And answered my soul and wept.

" Lyanna, I hoop thee with arms of fire ! "—
　　My voice was a hand of music that wrote,—
" Lyanna, my life is a single wire,
　　Thy love is its single note.
Hast thou known me thus ?　Shall it sound entire,
　　Full as the angels' who hover and harp
To the glory that 's God, like one golden lyre
　　　　Borne in a beam that is sharp ?　.　.　.

" Gladdened a splendor of rose, a splendor
  Out of the East : and the ruby bloom
Hiding—what, love?   Two eyes that are tender ?
  Two lips that are flame, and limbs of perfume
And fragrant fire ?—And who was the sender
    To thee of this lover ?"   .   .   .   And, bending
      low,
Spiritual my speech as a flower that, slender,
    Blooms when the wild stars blow.

Seemed all her passionate pulses to quicken ;
  Flowed all her soul to her eyes ; but sleep
Shadowed her voice ; and her voice seemed to
    thicken
  With sorrow that longed to weep :
" Yea, l divined thee, yea, and was stricken.
  Morn was my messenger-dove of love.
Alas !   I divined ; and I seemed to sicken,
    To perish and pine thereof.

" White are the clouds ; but I knew thee whiter
  In dazzling domes of the Dawn : I knew,
Though bright are God's stars, that thine eyes were
    brighter,
  Brighter and burning blue.
And my love was thine ; though it held thee
    slighter
  Than breezes bruiting it, murmuring by ;
And waited and yearned, and the yearning tighter
    Than tears in the hearts that die.

" ' Lyanna ! Lyanna ! ' thou calledst ever :
   ' Lyanna ! ' a ripple of rays that came :
' Lyanna, thy name is like song forever ! '
   And I marveled at my name.
The voice was such as if stars should sever
   For utt'rance of silver-syllabled beams :
' Lyanna ! Lyanna ! ' I turned, but never
      Informed thee more than my dreams.

" Thou walkedst a beauty afar : a glitter
   Of gleaming aroma : and I with moan
Flung thee mine arms : and thy gaze was bitter,
   Calmer and sterner than stone :
Avoiding thou passedst in scorn . . . oh, fitter
   The hate of all Heaven for me than this,
Thy scorn !—and I wept, when, oh, a flitter
      Of fire, a laugh, and a kiss ! " . . .

I had won her love. And the lungs of the thunder
   Trumpeted tempest ; and dark the seas
Lunged at the walls like a roaring wonder ;
   And the black rain buzzed like bees.—
Lyanna my bride. And the heavens asunder
   Rushed—chasms of glaring storm, where ran
The thunder's cataracts rolling under—
      For, behold ! her race was man.

Mine, of the elements. At the moth-white portal
   Of dreams stood the soul with her name. I saw
The glory and said, " Of the utterly mortal
   Mine the eternal lot and law !—

Thou lovest me ? "—" Yea ! dost thou question ? "—
   " Immortal
Am I through thy love, O Lyanna !" . . .
   'T is said,
Behold, when they came in the morn, a-startle
      Were lips with " Lyanna is dead !" .

MASKS.

Cucullus non facit monachum.

L IVE it down ! as you have spoken.
  You could live it ere you knew
What love was—"a bauble broken
Of a foolish thing untrue."—
You, Viola, with your beauty,
Cloistered, die a nun ?   No ; you—
You must live, and 't is your duty.

There 's your poniard ; for the second
In this tazza dropped ; the blood
On it scarcely hard.   I reckoned
Happily that hour we stood
There upon your palace stairway,
How, with the Franciscan hood
Cowled, I said, there was a bare way.

In the minster there I found it—
Your revenge.   I saw him wild
Stalking to the church ; around it
Dogged him, marking how he smiled
In the moonlight where he waited.
When the great clock beating dialed
Ten, I knew he would be mated.

Heaven or my better devil !—
Hardly had his sword and plume
Vanished in the dark, than, level
On the long lagune, did loom
Into moonlight-woven arches
Her slim gondola ; all gloom ;
One tall gondolier ; no torches.

Dusky gondolas kept bringing
Revellers ; and far the night
Rang with merriment and singing.—
From the imbricated light
Of the oar-vibrating water,
Gliding up the stairway, white,
Velvet-masked—the count's own daughter.

Quickly met her : whispered, " Flora,
Gaston.— *Mia*, till they go
One brief moment here, Siora."
She 'll perceive us—she below
With the duchess diamonds sparkling
Round th' inviolable glow
Of her throat—must pass us darkling :

" She 's Viola ! " .   .   .   And I drew her
In the old neglected pile—
Under her black mask I knew her,
By the chin, the lips, the smile.
Through the marble-foliated
Window fell the moonrays.   While
All the maskers passed we waited.

10

I had drawn the dagger. Turning
Called her by her name. Some lie
Of a passion sighed, her burning
Cheek on mine when, gliding by
In the light *his* form bejewelled
Gleamed. My very blood burned dry
With the hate his presence fueled.

My revenge: up-pushing slightly
Cowl, the mask fell and revealed
Balka as the poniard whitely
Flashed. The hollow nave re-pealed
One long shriek but once repeated.
Yet, I stabbed her thrice. She reeled
Dead. I thought of you, the heated

Horror on my hands, and tarried
Like the silence. Drawn aside
On her face the mask hung, married
To its camphor pallor: wide
Eyes with terror-stone. One second
I regretted, then defied
All remorse. Your promise beckoned,

And I left her. Love had pointed
Me this way. I walked the way
Clear-eyed and . . . it has anointed
Us fast lovers? will you say
Yes? or in despair go nun it
For this man who scorned you?—Nay!—
Live to hate him, you 've begun it.

THE SUCCUBA.

I HAVE dreams where I believe
   I am prince of some dim palace ;
One, at morn my Genevieve,
   Is at night the Lady Alice
Long, long dead, who was my bride :
And she glowers at my side
   Paly as a crystal chalice
Filled with fire diamond-dyed.

I have dreams and I shall die
   Wondering on them.   I remember
In my sleep her icy eye
   Draws me with its mournful ember
Up a castle's stairs that pave
Alabaster to the wave,
   Ghostly in the gray November ;
And my soul is all her slave.

Walls of shadow and of night
   Slit with casements full of fire,
Ruby or a piercing white :
   As the wind breathes lower, higher,

Round the towers spirit things
Whisper, and a moaning sings
    In the strings of each huge lyre
Set upon its four chief wings.

In its corridors at tryst
    Flame-eyed phantoms meet.   Its sparry
Halls are misty amethyst,
    Battlemented 'neath the starry
Skies of death that none has known ;
Heavens with the green stars sown
    Low and large, and all their barry
Beams blown on an ocean lone.

Can it be a witch is she
    Or a vampire, who is whiter
Than the spirits of the sea ?
    For my dreams inform her brighter
Than the faint foam-blossoms.   Lo,
All this passion is my foe !
    For her love lies tighter, tighter
On my heart than utter woe.

I but vaguely know I live
    Two pale lives of sweetest sorrow,
Where my love must give and give
    Passion, that its soul must borrow
Of the living, to the dead,
To the dear unhallowéd :
    And should I be death's to-morrow,
If I knew, I could not dread.

Lo, my dreams have drowned that place
  In all moon-white flowers : lilies
Like the influence of a face ;
  Knots of pearly amaryllis ;
Cactus-bulks with pulpy blooms
Puffy in the silver glooms ;
  White each hill with daffadillies
O'er the olive ocean looms.

But to me their fragrance seems
  Poison ; and their lambent lustre,
Spun of twilight and of dreams,
  Poison ; and each frosty cluster
Hides a serpent's fang, and I
Looking from an oriel, sigh ;
  For my soul doth ache to muster
Heart to breathe of them and die.

Then I feel big eyes as bright
  As the sea-stars. Gray with glitter
Glides unto me, clad in white,
  She. Deep hangings sway and flitter
Loves and deeds of Amadis
Darkly worked. And, lo, this is
  She the night brings, sweet and bitter
With a bliss that is not bliss.

And I kiss her eyes and hair ;
  Smooth her tresses till their golden
Glimmer sparkles. Everywhere
  Shapes of strange aromas, holden

Of her halls, about us troop
Foggy forms, that float and stoop,
   On slow swells of rolling, olden
Music, odorous loop in loop.

Still I see beneath it all—
   All this sorcery—a devil,
Beautiful and grandly tall,
   Broods with shadowy eyes of evil :
And I know, each lilac morn,
In that land a cactus-thorn,
   Monstrous on some lonely level,
Blooms for her I may not scorn.   .   .   .

I have dreams where I believe
   I am prince of some dim palace ;
One, at morn my Genevieve,
   Is at night the Lady Alice
Long, long dead.—Who may be brave,
Held and haunted of the grave ?
   When through some unholy malice
One a prince is and a slave.

BLODEUWEDD.

NOT to that demon's son, whom Arthur erst,
    For prophecy, at old Caerlleon durst
Grace wisely, Merlin,—not to him alone
Did those lost learnings of high magic, done
With mystery and marvels, then belong :
Taliesin, now, hath told us in a song
Of one at Arvon, Math of Gwynedd ; lord
Of some vague cantrevs of the North ; whose sword
Beat back and slew the monarch of the South
Through puissance of Gwydion.

                      His mouth
Was wise with wondrous witchcraft ; for his word
Wrought the invisible visible and stirred
Eyes with a seeming sight that, so deceived,
The mind conceited shapes and shapes believed :
Wrought flesh creations from air elements,
For, let him wish, the winds were wan with tents,
And brassy blasts of war from bugles brayed,
And armored hosts of battle clanged and swayed,
And at a word were not.   With little care
Steeds, rich-accoutred, and pied hounds, as fair,
Limber, and wiry as the dogs of Earth,
Fashioned from forest fungus, and gave birth

To lives of twice twelve hours, wherein they moved
Existences, and form perfections proved.

Now, to Caer Dathyl, Math through Gwydion,—
The son of Don,—the daughter dark of Don,
The silver-circled Arianrod, had brought :—
A southern rose of beauty, friendship sought
For full espousal. When the maiden came
Said Math, " Art thou a virgin ?" like a flame,
Mantling, her answer angered, "Verily,
I know not other, lord, than that I be !"
So wrought he then through magic that the form
Of her boy baby seemed upon her arm,
A chubby child.

                    " A Mary ?—Yea," laughed Math,
" Forsooth, another Mary !" then in wrath
Set harsh hands on the babe and fiercely flung
Far in the salt sea. But the hard winds clung
Fast to the Elfin and the lithe waves swept
Him safely shoreward dry. Some fishers kept
Him thus unseaed and christened Dylan, fair
Son of the Wave, and fostered him with care.

Nor really was this hers. But Gwydion,
Brother to Arianrod, before the sun
Had time to touch it with one golden glaive,
Some dim small body on the castle pave
In raven velvet seized ; and, hiding, he

Stole this from court, to subtly raise to be
A comely youth.   In time to Arianrod
Brought, swearing by the rood and blood of God
This was his sister's son.

      Quoth she : " More shame
Dost thou disgrace thee with to mix our name
With this dishonor, brother, than myself ! "
And, waxing wroth, cried Gwydion, " The Elf
Is thine?   God's curse ! " and daggered her with
  looks.
And she in turn waxed fiery saying, " Books
Of wisdom I have read as well as thou !
And, yea, upon thy folly, listen, now
I lay a threefold destiny : The first—
Until I name him, nameless is he !—Cursed
Be they who give him arms with palsy ! nor
Shall he bear such until I arm for war.
And, lastly, know, however high his birth,
He shall not wed a woman of the Earth !—
Malignity ! to shame me with thy sin ! "
So passed into her tower and locked her in.

But Gwydion, departing with the youth,
Sware he would compass her ; if not through truth,
Through wiles of learned magic.   And he wrought
So that unbending Arianrod was brought
To name the lad.   Again he managed that,
Through fierce enchantments as of war, he gat

Her to give arms.   But then, not for his life,
Howbeit, could he get the youth a wife.
Persisting desperate, anon the thing
Wrought in him blusterous as a backward spring.

Now Llew the youth was named.   And Gwydion
Made his complaint to Math, the mighty son
Of Mathonwy.
                        Said he : " Despair not.   We
By charms, illusions, and white sorcery
Will seek to make—for have we not such powers ?
—A woman for him out of forest flowers."

And so they toiled together one wan night,
When the gray moon hung low and watched, a
        white,
Wild witch's face behind a mist.   They took
Blossoms of briers by a bloomy brook
Shed from the April hills ; and phantom blooms
Of yellow broom that filtered faint perfumes ;
Thin, rare, frail primroses of rainy smell,
Weak pink, cirque-clustered in a glow-worm dell ;
Wild-apple sprigs that tipsied bells of blaze
And in far, haunted hollows made a haze
Of ghostly, fugitive fragrance ; plaintive blue
Of hollow harebells hoary with the dew ;
Kingcups as golden as the large, low stars ;
And lilies which, rolled limpid in long bars
Like sleepy starshine, swayed aslant and spilled
Slim nectar-cups of musk the rain had filled ;

And paly, wildwood windflowers, slight of gloss,
Dotting the oak-roots bulging up the moss ;
Lone on the Elfin uplands pulled the buds,
That burn like spurts of moonlight when it suds
The rainy clouds, of blossomed meadow-sweet,
And made a woman tall, from crown to feet
Complete in beauty.   One far lovelier
Than Branwen, daughter of the gray King Llyr ;
Than that dark daughter of Leodegrance,
The stately Gwenhevar.   And old romance
Dreamed in the open Bibles of her eyes ;
Music her motion ; and her speech, soft sighs
Of an acknowledged love for love again ;
And in her face no least suggested pain,
But hope, high heart, and happiness of life.

So Blodeuwedd they named her and as wife—
Fair aspect of wild flowers baptized with dew—
Gave that next morning to the happy Llew.

ACCOLON OF GAUL.

Prelude.

O WISEST legend from the storied wells
    Of lost Baranton ! where old Merlin dwells,
Nodding a white poll and a grave, gray beard,
As if some Lake Ladyé he, listening, heard,
Who spake like water, danced like careful showers
With blown gold curls through drifts of wild-thorn
    flowers ;
Loose, lazy arms upon her bosom crossed,
Float flower-like down a woodland vista ; lost
With one peculiar note that wrings a tear
Slow down his withered cheek.   And then steals
    near
A sweet, lascivious brow's white wonderment,
And gray, rude eyes, and hair which hath the scent
Of the wildwood Brécéliand's perfumes
In Brittany ; and in it one red bloom's
Blood-drop thrust deep ; and so " Sweet Viviane ! "
All the glad leaves lisp like a glad spring rain
From top to top, until a running surge
The dark witch-haunted solitude will urge,

That shakes and sounds and stammers as from
    sleep
Some giant were aroused ; and with a leap
A samite-hazy creature, blossom-white,
Showers mocking kisses down and, like a light
Beat by a gust to flutter and then done,
From Merlin and Brécéliande she's gone.
But still he sits there drowsing with his dreams,
A wondrous company ; as many as gleams
That stab the moted mazes of a beech ;
And each grave dream hath its own magic speech
To sting his old, sad eyes to tears—and two
Hang, tangled brilliants, in his beard like dew :
And far-off murmurs of courts brave and fair,
And forms of Arthur, stately Guenevere,
Tall Tristram and rare Isoud and stout Mark,
Bold Launcelot, chaste Galahad the dark
Of his weak mind, once strong, glares up with ;
    then,—
The instant's fostered blossoms—die again.
A roar of tournaments, a rippling stir
Of silken lists that ramble in to her,
That white, witch-mothered beauty, Viviane,
The vast Brécéliande and dreams again.
Then Dagonet, King Arthur's fool, stands there,
A waggish cunning ; glittering on his hair
A tinsel crown ; and then will slowly sway
Thick leaves and part, and there Morgane the Fay,
With haughty wicked eyes and lovely face,
Studies him steady for a little space.

I.

ACCOLON.

THOU speakest with thy questioning eyes again ;
   Here where the restless forest hears the main
Toss in a troubled sleep and moan and beat
A pensive passion out that woods repeat.

MORGANE.

And what wild beauty here ! where roughly run
Long forest shadows from the sinking sun,
The wood 's a subdued power gentle as
The tame wild-things that, in the moss and grass,
Gaze with their human eyes.   Here grow the lines
Of pale-starred green ; and where the fountain
      shines,
Urned in its tremulous ferns, let 's rest upon
This oak-trunk by the tempest overthrown
Years, years agone ; not where 't is rotted brown
But where the thick bark 's firm and overgrown
Of trailing ivy blackly berried ; where
Moist musk of wood decay just tincts the air,
As if a strange shrub on a whispering way,
In some wet dell, while dreaming of one May,
In longing languor weakly tried to wake
One sometime blossom and could only make
Ghosts of such dead aromas as it knew,
And shape a spectre, fragrant as thin dew,
To haunt these sounding miles of solitude.

ACCOLON.

Troubled thou speakest, Morgane, and the mood,
Unfathomed in thine eyes, glows ; rash and deep
As that in some wild woman's,—found asleep
By some lost knight upon a precipice,—
Whom he hath wakened with a laughing kiss.
As that of some frail elfin lady, light
As are the foggy moonbeams ; filmy white ;
Who waves diaphanous beauty on a cliff
That, drowsing, purrs with moon-drenched pines ;
     but if
The lone knight follow, foul fiends rise and drag
Him crashing down, while she, tall on the crag,
Triumphant, mocks him with glad sorcery
Till all the wildwood echoes shout with glee.—
As that bewildering mystery of a tarn,
A mountain water, which the mornings scorn
To anadem with fire and leave gray ;
To which a champion cometh when the Day
Hath tired of breding for the Twilight's head
Flame-flurry blooms, and golden-chapletéd,
Sits rosy, trembling with fierce love for Night,
Who cometh sandaled ; dark in crape ; the light
Of her good eyes a marvel ; her vast hair
Tortuous with stars,—as in a shadowy lair
The eyes of hunted wild things burn with rage,—
And on her bosom doth his love assuage :
He, coming heated to that haunted place,
Stoops down to lave his forehead, when his face

Meets gurgling fairy faces in a ring
That jostle upward ; babbling, beckoning
Him deep to wonders, magic built of old
For some dim witch—

MORGANE.

A city walled with gold,
With beryl battlements and paved with pearls,
Slim, lambent towers wrought of foamy swirls
Of alabaster ; and that witch to love,
More beautiful than any queen above !—

ACCOLON.

He pauses troubled ; but a wizard power,
In all his bronzen harness, that mad hour
Plunges him—whither?   What if he should miss
Those cloudy beauties and that creature's kiss ?—
Ah, Morgane, that same power Accolon
Saw potent in thine eyes and it hath drawn
Him onward—onward to what breathless fate ?

MORGANE.

Bliss.

ACCOLON.

Yea ; too true ! deep have we drank of late !
But there may come what stealthy-footed death
With bony claws to clutch away this breath ? . . .
I dreamed last night one culled wild flowers for me,

Larger than those of earth ; and I did see
Their woolly gold, loose, webby woven through,—
Like fluffy flames spun,—gauzy with fine dew :
And "Asphodels," I murmured ; then, "These
    sure
Are Eden amaranths, so angel pure
That love alone may pluck them aye and aye : "
When she had given, lo, she passed away
Beyond me, on a misty, yearning brook
With a sweet song, which all the wild air took
With torn farewells and pensive melody
Touching to tears, strange, hopeless utterly ;
So merciless sad that I yearned high to tear
Those ingot-cored and gold-crowned lilies there ;
Yet over me a horror which restrained
With melancholy presence of two pained
And awful, God-like eyes that cowed and held
Me weeping while that sad dirge died or swelled
Far, far on endless waters borne away :—
A wild bird's music, smitten when the ray
Of dawn it burned for graced its drooping head,
And the pale glory strengthened round it—dead ;
Daggered of thorns it plunged on, blind in night,
The slow blood ruby on its breast of white.—
And I—I knew the flowers which she had given
Were strays of parting grief and waifs of Heaven
For tears and memories ; too delicate,
For what is Earth's, her love immaculate !
But then—my God ! my God ! thus I was left,
And these were with me who was so bereft.

11

Oh, rapturous torment of a growing grief,
That weighed my soul who saw no near relief. . . .

And bowed and wept into his hands ; and she
Sorrowful beheld ; and resting at her knee
Raised slow her oblong lute and smote its chords ;
But ere the impulse saddened into words,
Said : " And didst love me as thy lips would prove,
No visions wrought of sleep might move thy love.
Firm is all Love in firmness of his power,
With flame reverberant moated stands his tower ;
Not so built as to chink from fact a beam
Of doubt and much less of a doubt from dream ;
Such, the alchemic fire of Love's desires, —
That fills its flaming moat,—melts to gold wires
To chord the old lyre new whereon he lyres."
So ceased ; and then, sad softness in her eye,
Sang to his dream a questioning reply :

" Will love grow less when dead the roguish
    Spring,
Who from gay eyes sowed violets whispering ?
Peach petals in wild cheeks, wan-wasted through
Of withering grief, laid lovely 'neath the dew,
          Will love grow less ?

" Will love grow less when comes queen Summer
    tall,
Her throat a lily, long and spiritual ?

Rich as the poppied swaths—hushed haunt of
    bees—
Her cheeks, a brown maid's gleaning on the leas,
        Will love grow less?

"Will love grow less when Autumn, sighing there,
Bends with long frost-streaks in her dark, dark
    hair?
Tears in grave eyes as in grave heavens above,
Deep lost in memories' melancholy, love,
        Will love grow less?

"Will love grow less when Winter at the door
Begs, on her thin locks icicles as hoar?
While Death's eyes, hollow o'er her shoulder,
    dart
A look to wring to tears then freeze the heart,
        Will love grow less?"

And in her hair wept softly, and her breast
Rose and was wet with tears; like as, distressed,
Night steals on Day rain sobbing through her
    curls.—

"Though tears become thee even as priceless pearls,
Weep not, oh, weep not!—Mine no gloom of doubt,
But woe for sweet love's death my dream brought
    out,"
He said. "Crowned, throned and flame-anointed, he
Kings our twin-kingdomed hearts eternally:

Love, high in Heaven beginning and to cease
No majesty when hearts are laid at peace ;
But reign supreme, if souls have wrought thus well,
A god in Heaven or a god in Hell."

So they communed.　And there her castle stood
With slender towers white above the wood ;
A forest lodge, in ivy buried, near ;
And woodland vistas, where faint herds of deer
Stalked like soft shadows ; where the roes did run,
Mavis and throstle caroled in the sun ;
And white waves marbled up a singing shore.
For it was Gore, Morgana's realm of Gore,
The white enchantress' Castle Chariot,
Where she her husband, Urience, forgot.

　　　.　　　.　　　.　　　.　　　.　　　.　　　.

Hurt in that battle where King Arthur strove
With the five heathen kings, and, slaying, drove
The five before him, Accolon, distraught,
To a white castle on his shield was brought,—
Wood-belted lawns melodious with birds,
Far from the rush of spears and roar of swords,—
By twelve dim damsels, tire maids of a queen
Stately and dark, who moved as if a sheen
Of starlight shone around her ; and who came
With healing herbs and searched his wounds.　A
　　　dame,
So beautiful in raiment silvery,
So white, that she attendant seemed to be

On that high holy Grael, which Arthur hath
Sought ever widely by wild wood and path ;—
Thus not for him, a worldly one to love,
Who loved her even to wonder ; skied above
His worship as the moon above the main,
That yearneth upward, passionate with pain,
And suffereth from weary year to year.
She peaceful pitiless with virgin cheer.

One night a tempest tossed and beat and lashed
The writhing forest and deep thunders dashed
Sonorous arms together ; and anon,
Between the thunder pauses, seas would groan
Like some enormous curse a knight hath lured
From where it soared to maim it with his sword.
And Accolon, in fever, seemed to see
The stormy, wide-wrenched night's eternity
Yawn hells of golden ghastliness ; and sweep
Distending foam tempestuous up each steep
Of raucous iron ; and nude mermaids sit
With tangled hair back-blown, and lightning-lit,
Sing wildly ; beckoning with naked arms
Some hurt barque strangled with the hurrying
    storm's
Resistless exultation.   And there came
One breaker mounting inward, all aflame
With glow-worm green, to boom against the cliff
Its thunderous bulk—and there, sucked pale and
    stiff,
Tumbled in eddies up the howling rocks,

His dead, drawn face ; eyes lidless ; matted locks
Oozed close with brine ; hurled upward flabbily
To streaming mermaids.   Madly seemed to see
The vampire echoes of the hoarse wood, who,
Collected, sought him : down the casement drew
Wet, shuddering, hag-like fingers ; thronging fast
Up hooting turrets blew an Elfin blast
For madder hunting, and whirled shouting off
On to the forest with a screaming scoff.—
Then, far away, hoofs of a hundred gales,
As wave rams wave up windy bluffs of Wales,
Loosed from the ancient hills, the cohorts loud,
Witches of tempest, clove the driven cloud,
And down the rocking night rolled, with the glare
Of goblin eyeballs burning ; their long hair
Blown, black with rain, unkempt from bony brows ;
Wide mouths of storm that yelled a Hell carouse,
Or bulged lean cheeks with wind ; rolled ruining
        by,
Headlong to roaring cliffs, to headlong die.

Once when the lightning made the casement glare
Squares touched to gold, between it rose her hair,
As if a raven's wing had cut the storm
Death-driven seaward.   And the vague alarm
Of her calm coming soothed his mind, as hope,
Surmising wings, assays to test their scope.
And now she kneeled beside him, beautiful,
White-raimented and white ; kneeled low,—" to
        lull

All thoughts of night such nights may bring to thee,
All such to peace and sleep."—Ah, God ! to see
Her like a living benediction near !
To hear her voice ! her cool hand smoothing here,
Wistful, his feverish brow and deep dark curls !
To see her rich throat's carcaneted pearls
Rise with her breathing ! eyes' pure influence
Poured toward him straight as stars, whose sole
    defence
Against all storm is their bold beauty ! then
To feel her breath and hear her voice again !—
" Love, mark," he said or dreamed he moaned in
    dreams,
" How bursts the tumult and the thunder gleams !—
Nay, Arthur's knights have charged on battle fields
Of Humber ! fiery spears and fiery shields
Have flashed and fall'n ! the five fierce kings are
    down !
The rush of onset hurls, and night comes on . . .
Love, one eternal tempest thus with thee
Were calm, deep calm ! But, no! through thee for me
Such calm proves tempest. Speak ; I feel thy voice,
A hush caressing silence, healing noise."

" And thou—thou lov'st my voice? fond Accolon !
Why not—yea, why not ?—Nay ! I prithee, groan
Not for . . . what more hast had long since
    thine all ?"—
She smiled ; and dashed down storm's black-crum-
    bled wall,

Baptizing moonlight bathed her, foot and face
Deluging, as his soul turned toward her grace
With worship from despair and secret grief . . .
And that immortal night to him she said
Words, lay he white in death had raised him red.

" Now rest," she said, "I love thee with much
        love !—
Some speak of secret love, but God above
Hath knowledge and divinement. Winds may
    - blow ;
To lie by thee to-night my mind is ; so,"—
She laughed,—" sleep well ! For me, but thy fast
        word
Of knighthood, look thou, and thy naked sword
Laid in betwixt us . . .   Let it be a wall
Strong between love and lust and lov'st me all in
        all."
Undid the goodly gold from her clasped waist ;
Unbound deep locks ; and, like a blossom faced,
Stood sweet an unswayed stem that ran to bud
In breasts and face a graceful womanhood :
And fragrance was to her as natural
As odor to the rose ; and she a tall
White ardor and white fervor in the room
Moved, some pale presence that with light doth
        bloom.
And all his eyes and lips and limbs were fire ;
His tongue, delirious, babbled of " desire " ;
How hers was devil's kindness, which is even

More than fiend's fury, since the soul sees Heaven,
Among eternal torments unforgiven :
Temptation harbored, like a bloody rust
On a bright blade, leaves ugly stains : how lust
Is love's undoing when love's limbs are cast
Naked before desire : what love so chaste
But this warm nearness of what should be hid
Makes it a lawless love ?—" But thou hast bid.
Rest thou. I love thee, love thee as I know ;
And all my love doth battle with love's foe ! "

Then she, as pure as snows of peaks that keep
Sun-cloven crowns of virgin-steadfast steep,
Frowned on him, and the thoughts, that in his
        brain
Had risen a glare of gems, set dull as rain,
As one high look she gave of grief and pain.
He, turning, sighed into his hands ; and she
Stretched the broad blade's division suddenly.

And so they lay its iron between them twain :
Unsleeping he, for all the brute disdain
Of passion in him struggled up and stood
A rebel wrangling with the brain and blood.
An hour stole by : she slept or seemed to sleep.
The winds of night came vigorous from the deep
With rain scents of storm-watered field and wold,
And breathed of ocean meadows bluely rolled.
He drowsed ; and time passed stealing as for one
Whose easy life dreams in Avilion.

Vast bulks of black, wind-shattered rack went down
High casement squares of heaven, a crystal crown
Of bubbled moonlight on each giant head,
Like as great ghosts of Cornwall kings long dead.
And then he thought she lightly laughed and sighed,
So soft a taper had not bent aside,
And leaned a soft face, seen through loosened hair,
Above him, whisp'ring as one speaks in prayer,
" Behold, the sword !   I take the sword away ! "

It curved and clashed where the strewn rushes lay ;
Shone glassy, glittering like a watery beam
Of moonlight in the moonlight.   He did deem
She moved in sleep and dreamed perverse, nor wist
That which she did until two fierce lips kissed
His wondering eyes to wakement of her thought.
Then said he, "Love, my word ! is it then naught ? "
But now he felt her kisses over and over,
And laughter of, " What is thy word, my lover ?
Thy word, if she, to whom thou gavest it,
Unbind thee of it ?   lo, and she sees fit ! "

II.

N OON ; and the wistful Autumn sat among
       The lurid woodlands ; chiefs who now were
          wrung
By crafty ministers, sun, wind and frost,
To don imperial pomp at any cost.

On each wild hill they stood as if for war,
Flaunting barbaric raiment wide and far;
And burnt-out lusts in aged faces raged;
Their tottering state by flattering zephyrs paged,
Who in a little fretful while, how soon !
Would work rebellion under some wan moon ;
Pluck their old beards ; deriding, shriek, and tear
Rich royalty ; sow tattered through the air
Their purple majesty ; and from each head
Dash down its golden crown, and in its stead
Set there a pale-death mockery of snow,.
Leave them bemoaning beggars bowed with woe.

Wild blare of horns and snapping of steel bows—
A mort ! a mort !—the hunt is up and goes,
Beneath the acorn-dropping oaks, in green,—
Dark woodland green,—a boar-spear held between
His selle and hunter's head, and at his thigh
A good broad hanger, and one hand on high
To wind the rapid echoes from his horn,
That scare the field-birds from the sheavéd corn.
Away, away they flash, a belted band
From Camelot, through that haze-haunted land ;
Hounds leashed and leamers and a sheen of steel,
A tramp of horse and the bell-baying peal
Of coupled stag-hounds and—the hart ! the hart,
A lordly height, doth from the covert dart ;
And the big blood-hounds bound unto the chase.
A hunt ! a hunt ! the pryce seems but a pace
On ere 't is wound. But now, where interlace

The dense-briered underwoods, the dogs have lost
The slot, there where a forest brook hath crossed
With intercepting water full of leaves.

Beyond, the hart a tangled labyrinth weaves
Through dimmer boscage ; and the wizard sun
Shapes many shadowy stags that seem to run
Wild herds before the baffled foresters.
And, treed aloft, a reckless laugh one hears,
As if some helping goblin of the trees
Mocked them the unbayed hart and made a breeze
His pursuivant of mocking.   Hastening thence,
Pursued King Arthur and King Urience,
With one small brachet, till scarce hear could they
Their fellowship, far distant, ride away.
And there the hart plunged bravely through the
        brake,
Leaving a torn path shaking in his wake,
Down which they followed on through many a
        copse,
Above whose brush, close on before, the tops
Of the stag's antlers swelled anon, and so
Were gone where beat the brambles to and fro.
And still they drave him hard ; and ever near
Seemed that great hart unwearied ; and such cheer
Still stung them to the chase.   When Arthur's
        horse
Gasped mightily and, lunging in his course,
Lay dead, a lordly bay ; and Urience
Reined his gray hunter laboring.   And thence

King Arthur went afoot. When suddenly
He was aware of a wide waste of sea,
And near the wood the hart upon the sward
Bayed, panting unto death and winded hard.
And so the king dispatched him and the pryce
Wound on his golden hunting-bugle thrice.

As if each echo, which that wild horn's blast
Roused from its sleep,—the quietude had cast
Tender as mercy on it,—in a band
Rose moving sounds of gladness hand in hand,
Came twelve fair damsels, sunny in sovereign
      white,
From the red woodland gliding. They the knight
Graced with obeisance ; and " Our lord," said one,
" Tenders you courtesy until the dawn ;
The Earl Sir Damas. Well in his wide keep,
Seen thither with due worship, you shall sleep."
And so he came o'erwearied to a hall,
An owlet-haunted pile, whose weedy wall
Towered based on crags ; rough turrets, crowding
      high,—
An old gaunt giant-castle,—'gainst a sky
Wherein the moon hung owl-faced, gray and full.
Down on dark sea-foundations broke the dull
Vast monotone of ocean, and unrolled
The windy wilderness that was as old
As the defiant headlands, stretching out
Into the night, with their voluminous shout
Of wreck and wrath forever. Arthur then

Among the gaunt Earl's bandits, swarthy men,
Ate in the wild hall.   Then a damsel led
The king with flaring lamp unto his bed
Down lonely corridors of that old keep ;
And soon he rested in a heavy sleep.   .   .   .

And   then   King   Arthur   woke,   and   woke 'mid
    groans
Of dolorous knights ; and 'round him lay the bones
Of many woful champions mouldering ;
And he could hear the open ocean fling
Its booming waves above.   And so he thought,
" It is some nightmare weighing me, distraught
By that long hunt ; " and then he sought to shake
The horror off and to himself awake ;
But still he heard sad groans and whispering sighs ;
And deep in iron-ribbéd cells the eyes
Of pale, cadaverous knights shone fixed on him,
Unhappy ; and he felt his senses swim
With foulness of the cell ; cried, " What are ye ?
Ghosts of chained champions or a company
Of phantoms, bodiless fiends ?   If speak ye can,
Speak, in God's name ! for I am here—a man ! "
Then groaned the shaggy throat of one who lay
A dusky nightmare dying day by day,
Yet once of comely mien and strong withal
And greatly gracious ; but, now hunger-tall,
A scrawny ghost with faded hands and cheeks :
" Sir knight," said he, " know that the wretch who
    speaks

Is but an one of twenty knights here shamed
By him who lords this castle, Damas named,
Who mews us here for slow starvation.   Seen
Around you, rot the bones of some eighteen
Tried knights of Britain.   And God grant that
        soon
My hunger-lengthened ghost may see the moon
Beyond the famine of this prisonment."
With that he sighed, and down the dungeon went
A rustling sigh, like saddened sin, and so
Another dim, thin voice complained their woe :—

" He doth enchain us with this common end :
That he find one who will his prowess bend
To the attainment of this livelihood.
A younger brother, Ontzlake, hath he ; good
And courteous, withal most noble, whom
This Damas hates—yea, ever seeks his doom ;
Denying him to their estate all right
Save that he holds by main of arms and might.
Through puissance hath Ontzlake some fat fields
And one right sumptuous manor, where he yields
Belated knights all hospitality.
Then bold is Ontzlake, Damas cowardly.
For Ontzlake would decide by sword and lance,
Body to body, this inheritance ;
But Damas, vile as he is courageless,
Must on all guests perforce lay such distress,
To fight for him or starve.   For you must know
That in his country he is hated so

That no helm here is who will take the fight.
Thus fortunes it our plight is such a plight,"
Quoth he and ceased. And wondering at the tale
The king was thoughtful ; and each wasted, pale,
Poor countenance perused him while he spake :
" And what reward if one this cause should
    take ?"—
" Deliverance for all if of us one
Consent to be his party's champion.
But treachery and he are so close kin
We loathe the part as some misshapen sin ;
And here would rather with the rats find death
Than, serving falseness, save and shame our
    breath."

" May God deliver you in mercy, sirs ! "—
And right anon an iron noise he hears
Of chains rushed loose and bars jarred rusty back,
The heavy gate croak open. And the black
Of the rank cell astonished was with light,
That danced fantastic with the frantic night.
One high torch, sidewise worried by the gust,
Sunned that dark den of hunger, death and rust,
And one tall damsel vaguely vestured, fair
With shadowy hair, poised on the rocky stair.
And laughing on the King, " What cheer?" said
    she ;
" God's life, the keep stinks vilely ! And to see
These noble knights endungeoned, starving here,
Doth pain me sore with pity. But, what cheer ?"

" Thou mockest us. For me, the sorriest
Since I was suckled ; and of any quest
To me the most imperiling and strange.—
But what wouldst thou ?" said Arthur. She, " A
   change
I offer thee ; through thee to these with thee,
If thou dost promise, in love's courtesy,
To fight for Damas and his livelihood.
And if thou wilt not—look ! behold this brood
Of lean and dwindled bellies, famine-eyed,—
Keen knights once,—who refused me. So decide."

Then thought the King of the sweet sky, the breeze
That blew delicious over waves and trees ;
Thick fields of grasses and God's sunny earth,
Whose beating heat filled the red heart with mirth,
And made the world one sovereign pleasure-house
Where king and serf might revel and carouse ;
Then of the hunt on autumn-plaintive hills ;
Lone forest lodges by the radiant rills ;
His palace at Caerlleon upon Usk,
And Camelot's loud halls that through the dusk
Blazed far and bloomed a rose of revelry
Or in the misty morning shadowy
Loomed grave for audience. And then he thought
Of his Round Table and the Grael wide sought
In haunted holds by many a haunted shore ;
Then marveled of what wars would rise and roar
With dragon heads unconquered and devour
This realm of Britain and crush out that flower

12

Of chivalry whence ripened his renown ;
And then the reign of some besotted crown,
A bandit king of lust, idolatry—
And with that thought for tears he could not see.—
Then of his greatest champions, King Ban's son,
And Galahad and Tristram, Accolon ;
And then, ah God ! of his loved Guenevere :
And with the thought—to starve 'mid horrors
    here ?—
For, being unfriend to Arthur and his Court,
Well knew he this grim Earl would bless that sport
Of fortune which had fortuned him so well
To have his King to starve within a cell,
In the entombing rock beside the deep.—
And all the life shut in his limbs did leap
Through eager veins and sinews, fierce and red,
Stung on to action, and he rose and said :
" That which thou askest is right hard, but, lo !
To rot here harder.   I will fight his foe.
But, mark, I have no weapons and no mail,
No steed against that other to avail."

" Fear not for that ; and thou shalt lack none,
    sire."—
And so she led the way : her torch's fire
Scaring wild spidery shadows at each stride
From cob-webbed coignes the scowling arches hide.
At length they reached an iron-studded door,
Which she unlocked with one harsh key she bore
'Mid many keys bunched at her girdle ; thence

They issued on a terraced eminence.
Beneath, the sea broke sounding ; and the King
Breathed open air that had the scent and sting
Of brine morn-vigored and blue-billowed foam ;
And in the east the second dawning's gloam,
Since that unlucky chase, was freaked with streaks
Red as the ripe stripes of an apple's cheeks.
And so within that larger light of dawn
It seemed to Arthur now that he had known
This maiden at his court, and so he asked.
But she, well tutored, her real person masked,
And answered falsely, " Nay, deceive thee not.
Thou saw'st me ne'er at Arthur's court, I wot.
For here it likes me best to sing and spin
And work the hangings olden halls within.
No courts or tournaments to so enslave,
No knights to flatter me !   For me—the wave,
The forest, field and sky ; the calm, the storm ;
My garth wherein I walk to think ; the charm
Of uplands redolent at bounteous noon
And full of sunlight ; night's free stars and moon ;
White ships that pass some several every year ;
These lonesome towers and yon wild mews to hear."
" An owlet maid," the King laughed.—But untrue
Was she, and of false Morgane's treasonous crew,
Who worked strange wiles ev'n to the slaying of
The King, half-brother, whom she did not love.—
And presently she brought him where in state
This swarthy Damas 'mid mailed cowards sate.

.   .   .   .

And Accolon, at Castle Chariot still,
Had lost long months in love.   Her husband ill,
Morgane, perforce, must leave her lover here
Among the hills of Gore.   A lodge stood near
A cascade in the forest, where their wont
Was to sit listening the falling fount,
That, through sweet talks of many idle hours
On moss-banks languid with the violet flowers,
Had learned a laughing language thus thereof,
And wandered ever gently whispering "love":
Below the lodge it pooled into a well,
And slipping thence through dripping shadows fell
From rippling rock to rock.   Here Accolon,
With Morgane's hollow lute, each studious dawn
Came all alone ; not ev'n her brindled hound
To bound beside him o'er the gleaming ground ;
No handmaid lovely of his loveliest fair,
Or paging dwarf in purple with him there ;
But this her lute, about which her perfume
Clung odorous of memories, that made bloom
Her flower-features rosy at his eyes,
That saw soft words, his sense could but surmise,
Shaped on dim, breathing lips ; the laugh that drunk
Her deep soul-fire from eyes wherein it sunk
And slowly waned away to smouldering dreams,
Fathomless with thought, far in their dove-gray
          gleams.
And so for those most serious eyes and lips,
Faint, filmy features, all the music slips
Of buoyant passion bubbling to his voice

To chant her praises ; and with nervous poise
His fleet trained fingers call from her long lute
Such riotous notes as must make envy-mute
The nightingale that listens quivering.
And well he knows that winging hence it 'll sing
These aching notes, whose beauties burn and pain
Its anguished heart now sobless, not in vain
Beneath her casement in that garden old
Dingled with heavy roses ; in the gold
Of Camelot's stars and pearl-encrusted moon ;
And if it dies, the heartache of the tune
Shall clamor stormy farewells at her ear,
Of death more dear than life if love be near ;
Melt her quick eyes to tears, her throat to sobs,
That vanquish her, while separation throbs
Hard at her heart, and longing lifts to Death
Two prayerful eyes of pleading, "for one breath —
An instant of fierce life—crushed in his arms
Close, close ! And, oh, for such take thou my
    charms,
That have thus lived, to be thine evermore ! "
And sweet to know that every vow shall soar
Ev'n to the dull ear of her drowsy lord
Beside her ; heart-defiant as each word
Harped in the bird's voice rhythmically clear.
And thus he sang to her who was not near :—

  "She comes ! her presence, like a moving song
    Breathed soft of loveliest lips and lute-sweet
      tongue,

Sways all the gurgling forest from its rest :
I fancy where her rustling foot is pressed,
So faltering, love seems timid, but how strong
    The darling love that flutters in her breast !

"She comes ! and wildwood vistas are stormed
        through—
As if wild wings, wet-varnished with the dew,
    Had flashed a sudden sunbeam-tempest past,
    —With her eyes' inspiration, deeply chaste ;
A rhythmic lavishment of bright gray blue,
    Long arrows of her eyes perfection cast.

"O Love, she comes ! O Love, I feel thy breath,
Like the soft South that idly wandereth
    Through musical leaves of laughing laziness,
    Page on before her, how sweet —none can guess !
To say my soul, ' Here's harmony dear as death,
    To sigh wild vows or, utterless, to bless.'

" She comes, O Life ! and all thy brain is brave
To war for words to laud her and to lave
    Imperial beauty in such vows whereof
    Should hush melodious cooings of a dove :
For her light feet the favored path to pave
    With oaths, like roses, raving mad with love.

" She comes ! in me a passion—as the moon
Works madness in strong men—my blood doth
        swoon

Unto her glory ; and I feel her soul
Cling lip to lip with mine ; and now the whole
Mix with me, aching like a tender tune
Exhausted, lavished in a god's control.

" She comes ! ah, God ! ye eager stars that grace
The fragmentary skies, that dimple space,
   Fall, and I hear her harp-sweet footfalls come.
   Ah, wood-indulging, violet-vague perfume,
Art of her presence, of her wild-flower face,
   That, like some gracious blossom, stains the
      gloom ?

" Oh, bounding exultation of the blood !
That now—as sunbursts, (the almighty mood
   Of some moved god,) scatter the storm that roars,
   And hush—her love, like some spent splendor,
      pours
Into with all immaculate maidenhood ;
   And all the heart that hesitates—adores.

" Vanquished, sweet victor and triumphant sweet !
The height of heaven—supine at thy feet,
   Where love feasts crowned, and basks, in such
      a glare
   As cores of moons burn, in thine eyes and hair,
Unutterable with raveled fires that cheat
   The ardent clay of me and make me air.

" And so, rare witch, thy blood, like some lewd
　　wine,
Shall subtly make me, like thee, half divine ;
　　And—sweet rebellion—so defy and urge
　　Thee on to combat with a kiss, nor dirge
The war, that rubies all thy proud cheeks' shine
　　With struggling blushes, till white truce emerge.

" My life for thine, surrendered lip to lip :
A striving being pulsant, that shall slip,
　　Like song and flame, in sense from thee to me :
　　Nor kept, but quick surrendered back to thee ;
So our two loves live as a singleship,
　　Ten thousand loves as one eternally."

III.

THE evening came : long shadows cowled the way
　　Like sombre pilgrims who have kneeled to pray
Beside a wayside shrine ; and, rosy-rolled
Up th' amaranthine west, a stormy gold
Towered battlements far up the opal skies,
Which seemed to open gates of Paradise
On rushing hinges of the winds, and blaze
God's glory far 'mid melodies of praise.
And from the sunset, down the roseate ways,
To Accolon, who with his idle lute,
Reclined in revery against the root
Of a great oak, a fragment of the west,
A dwarf, in crimson satin tightly dressed,

Skipped like a leaf the rather frosts have burned
And cozened to a fever red, that turned
And withered all its sap. And this one came
From Camelot ; from his belovéd dame,
Morgane the Fay. He on his shoulder bore
A burning blade wrought strange with wizard lore
Of mystic runes ; within a scabbard, which
Glared venomous, with angry jewels rich.
He, louting to the knight, "Sir knight," said he,
"Your lady with all sweetest courtesy
Assures you—ah, unworthy messenger
I of such beauty !—of that love of her."
Then doffing the great baldric, with the sword
To him he gave : "And this from him, my lord
King Arthur ; even his Excalibur,
The Elfin blade which Merlin gat of her,
The Ladye of the Lake, who Launcelot
Fostered from infanthood, as well you wot,
In some weird mere in Briogne's tangled lands
Of charms and mist ; where filmy fairy bands
By lazy moons of autumn spin their fill
Of giddy morrice on the frosty hill.
By goodness of her favor this is sent,
Who craved King Arthur boon with this intent :
That soon for her a desperate combat, one
'Gainst one of mightier prowess, were begun ;
And with the sword Excalibur right sure
Were she against that champion to endure.—
The blade is trenchant, but guard thou the sheath,
Which, belting, saves the wearer from all death."

He said : and Accolon looked on the sword,
A fiery falchion ; said, " It shall go hard
With him through thee, unconquerable blade,
Who e'er he be, who on my Queen hath laid
Insult or injury: and hours as slow
As palsied hours in Purgatory go
For those unmassed, till I have slain this foe !—
Thy guerdon, page.—And now, to her who gave,
Dispatch ! and this : To all commands—her slave,
To death obedient.   In love or war
Her love to make me all the warrior.
Plead her grace mercy for so long delay
From love that dies an hourly death each day
Till her white hands kissed he shall kiss her face,
By which his life breathes in continual grace."
Thus he commanded.   And incontinent
The dwarf departed like a red shaft sent,
From clouds in uniforms of scarlet light
Ranked o'er long, purple glooms.   And with the
          night,
Whose votaress cypress stoled the dying strife
Softly of day, and for whose perished life
Gave heaven her golden stars, in dreamy thought
Wends Accolon to Castle Chariot.   .   .   .

And it befell that, wandering one dawn,
As was his wont, across a dew-drenched lawn,
Glad with night freshness and elastic health
In sky and earth, that lavished worlds of wealth

From heady winds and racy scents,—a knight
And lofty lady met him ; gay bedight,
With following of six esquires ; and they
Held on straight wrists the jess'd gerfalcon gray,
And rode a-hawking o'er the leas of Gore
From Ontzlake's manor, where he languished ; sore
Hurt in the lists, a spear wound in his thigh :
Who had besought—for much he feared to die—
This knight and his fair lady, as they rode
To hawk near Chariot, Morgane's abode,
That they would beg her in all charity
To come to him, (for in chirurgery
Of all that land she was the greatest leach,)
And her for his recovery beseech.
So, Accolon saluted, they drew rein,
And spake their message,—for right overfain
Were they toward their sport,—that he might bear
Petition to that lady.   But, not there
Was Arthur's sister, as they well must wot ;
But now a se'nnight lay at Camelot
The guest of Guenevere ; and with her there
Four other queens of farther Britain were :
Isoud of Ireland, she of Cornwall Queen,
King Mark's wife,—who right rarely then was
      seen
At Court for jealousy of Mark, who knew
Her to that lance of Lyonesse how true
Since mutual quaffing of a philter ; while
How guilty Guenevere on such could smile :—
She of Northgales and she of Eastland ; and

She of the Out Isles Queen. A fairer band
For sovereignty and love and loveliness
Was not in any realm to grace and bless.
Then quoth the knight, "Ay? see how fortune
    turns
And varies like an April day, that burns
Now welkins blue with calm, now scowls them
    down,
Revengeful, with a black storm's wrinkled frown.
For, look, this Damas, who so long hath lain
A hiding vermin, fearful of all pain,
Dark in his bandit towers by the deep,
Wakes from a five years' torpor and a sleep,
And sends dispatch a courier to my lord
With, ' Lo ! behold ! to-morrow with the sword
Earl Damas by his knight, at point of lance,
Decides the issue of inheritance,
Body to body, or by champion.'
Right hard to find such ere to-morrow dawn.
Though sore bestead lies Ontzlake, and he could,
Right fain were he to save this livelihood."

Then thought Sir Accolon : " Th' adventure goes
Even as Morgane hath messengered. Who knows
But what this battle is for her dear sake?"
Then said to those : " His quarrel I will take,—
If he be so conditioned, harried of
Estate and life,—in knighthood and for love.
Conduct me thither." With gramercies then
Mounted a void horse of that wondering train,

And thence departed with two squires. And they
Came to a lone, dismantled priory
Hard by a castle on whose square gray towers,
Machicolated, o'er the forest's bowers,
The immemorial morning bloomed and blushed :
A woodland manor, old and deep-embushed
In wild and woody hills. And then one wound
An echoing horn, and with the savage sound
The drawbridge rumbled moatward, clanking, and
Into a paved court passed the little band. . . .

When all the world was morning, gleam and glare
Of far deluging glory, and the air
Sang with the wood-bird, like a silver lyre
Swept swift of minstrel fingers, wire on wire,
Ere that fixed hour of prime, came Arthur armed
For battle royally. A black steed warmed
A keen impatience 'neath him ; huge in mail
Of foreign make ; accoutred head and tail
In costly sendal ; rearward wine-dark red,
Amber as sunlight to his fretful head.
Blue armor of knit links had Arthur on,
Beneath a robe of honor made of drawn,
Ribbed satin, diapered and purflewed deep
With lordly golden purple ; whence did sweep
Two hanging acorn-bangles of fine gold ;
And at his thigh a falchion, long and bold
And triple-edged ; its rune-stamped scabbard, of
Red leather, a rich baldric held above
Of new cut deer-skin ; this, laborious wrought

And curiously, with slides of gold was fraught,
And buckled with a buckle white that shone,
Bone of the seahorse, tongued with jet-black bone :
And, sapphire-set, a burgonet of gold
Whereon a wyvern sprawled, whose wide throat
    rolled
A flame-red tongue of agate, and whose eyes
Glowed venomous, rich rubies of great prize :
And in his hand a wiry lance of ash,
Lattened with finest silver, like a flash
Of sunlight, made an ever-twinkling gash.
A squire attended ; a tall youth whose head
Waved jaunty with close curls, whereon a red
Long-feathered cap was ; 'neath which eyes, as
    keen
As a wild-hawk's, and auburn beard were seen ;
His legs in hose of rarest Totness clad ;
And parti-colored leather shoes he had,
Gold-latched ; and in his hand a bannered spear,
Speckled and bronzen, sharpened in the air.

So with his following, while lay like scars
The blue mist thin along the woodland bars,
Through dew and fog, through shadow and through
    ray,
Joustward Earl Damas led the forest way.
Then to King Arthur, when arrived were these
Where lofty lists shone silken through the trees,
Bannered and draped, a wimpled damsel came,
Secret, upon a palfrey all aflame

With sweat and heat of hurry, and, "From her,
Your sister Morgane, your Excalibur,
With tender greeting. For you well may need
Him in this strange adventure. So God speed !"
Said and departed suddenly : nor knew
The King but this his weapon tried and true :
But brittle this and fashioned like thereof,
And false of baser metal,—in unlove
And treason to his life,—from her of kin
Half sister, who thought sure that she would win.

Then heralded into the lists he rode.
Opposed flashed Accolon, whose strength bestrode,
Exultant, proud in talisman of that sword,
A dun horse lofty as a haughty lord,
Pure white about each small, impatient hoof :
And knight and steed shone clad in arms of proof
Of yellow-dappled, variegated plate
Of Spanish laton. And of sovereign state
His surcoat robe of honor, white and black,
Of satin, red-silk needled front and back
Then crimson bordered : and above this robe
His two-edged sword,—a throbbing golden globe
Of vicious jewels,—thrust its splendid hilt ;
Its broad belt, tawny and with goldwork gilt,
Clasped with the eyelid of a black sea-horse
Whose tongue was rosy gold. And stern as Force
His visored helmet burned like fire, of rich
And bronzen laton hammered ; and on which
An hundred crystals glittered, thick as on

A silver web bright-studding dews of dawn ;
The casque's tall crest a taloned griffin ramped,
In whose horned head one virtuous gem was
     stamped.
An ashen spear, round-shafted, overlaid
With azure silver, whereon colors played,
Firm in his iron gauntlet lithely swayed.

Intense on either side an instant stood
Glittering as serpents that, with spring renewed,
In glossy scales meet on a grassy way,
Advance with angry tongues at poisonous play.
Then clanged a herald's clarion, and sharp heels,
Harsh-thrust, each champion's springing courser
     feels
Spur to red onset.   The adventured spears
Flashed, like swift sunbursts of a storm when clears
The adverse thunder ; and in middle course
Shrieked shrill the unpierced shields ; mailed horse
     from horse
Lashed madly pawing—and a hoarse roar rang
From tossing lists, till the wild echoes rang
Of league on league of forest and of cliff.
Rigid the champions rode where, standing stiff,
Their squires tendered them the spears they held ;
Nor stayed to breathe ; but, scarcely firmly selled,
Rushed fiery forward shield to savage shield ;
Opposing crest to crest ; the wyvern reeled
Toward the towering griffin ; scorn and scath
Glaring undaunted in the rocking wrath

Of balls of jeweled eyes, they raged and stood,
Slim, slippery symbols, in the sun like blood.
The lance of Accolon, as on a rock
The storm-launched foam breaks baffled, with the
     shock
On Arthur's sounding shield burst splintered force ;
But him resistless Arthur's,—high from horse
Uplifted,—headlong bare, and crashed him down,
A long sword's length unsaddled. Accolon
For one stunned moment lay. Then rising drew
The great sword at his hip that shone like dew
Sun-brushed with morn. " Descend," he stiffly
     said,
" To proof of better weapons, head for head !
Enough of spears ; to swords !" And so the knight
Addressed him to the King. Dismounting, white
His moon-bright brand the King unsheathed ; and
     high
Each covering shield gleamed slanting to the sky,
Relentless, strong and stubborn ; underneath
Their wary shelters foined the glittering death
That fenced and thrust ; one tortoise shield de-
     scends ;
A fierce blade leaps,—shrill as a flame that sends
A long fang heavenward, or a battle word,—
Swings hard and trenchant and, resounding heard,
Burns surly helmward full ; again each sword
Bounds to a brother blow to crash again
Blade on brave blade. And o'er the battered
     plain,

13

Over and over, blade on baleful blade ;
Teeth clenched ; behind hot visors eyes that made
A cavernous, smouldering fury ; shield at shield,
Unflinchingly remained and scorned to yield.

And Arthur drew aside to rest upon
His falchion for a space.　But Accolon
As yet, through virtue of that magic sheath
Fresh and almighty, being no nearer death
Through loss of blood than when the trial begun,
Chafed with delay.　But Arthur with the sun,
His heavy mail, the loss from wounds of blood,
Leaned over weary and so resting stood ;
When Accolon cried sneering, " Dost thou rest,
O woman ?" and hard on King Arthur pressed ;
" Defend thee ! yield thee ! or die recreant ! "
Full on his helm a hewing blow did plant,
That beat a flying fire from the steel.
Stunned, like one drunk with wine, the king did reel
Breath, brain-bewildered.　Then, infuriate,
Nerve-stung with vigor by that blow, in hate
Gnarled all his strength into one blow of might,
And in both fists the huge blade knotted tight
And swung, terrific with the coming stroke,—
As some swift light that hurls the riven oak,—
Boomed on the beaten burgonet he wore ;
Hacked through and through the crest, and cleanly
　　　　shore
The golden boasting of its griffin, fierce
With hollow clamor, down astounded ears.

No further thence—but shattered to the grass,
That brittle blade, crushed as if made of glass,
Into hot pieces like a broken ray
Burst sunward and in feverish fragments lay.
Then groaned the King unarmed. And then he
  knew
This no Excalibur, so tried and true,
And perfect tempered, runed and mystical !
He sobbed, " Morgane betrays me ! "—for withal
Him seemed this foe, who fought with so much
  stress,
So long untiring, and with no distress
Of wounds or heat, through treachery bare his
  brand ;
And then he knew it by the hilt his hand
Clutched for an avenging stroke. For Accolon
In madness urged the belted battle on
His King defenceless ; who, the hilted cross
Of that false weapon grasped, beneath the boss
Of his deep-dented shield crouched ; and around
Crawled the unequal conflict o'er the ground,
Sharded with shattered spears and blow-hewn bits
Of shivered steel and gold that burnt in fits.
So hunted, yet defiant, cowering
Beneath his shield's defence, the dauntless king
Persisted stoutly. And, devising still
How to secure his sword and by what skill,
Him thus it fortuned when most desperate :
In that close chase they came where, shattered late,
Lay tossed the truncheon of a bursten lance,

Which, deftly seized, to Accolon's advance
He wielded valorous.   Against the fist
Smote where the gauntlet husked the nervous wrist,
Which strained the weapon for a wrathful blow ;
Palsied, the tightened sinews of his foe
Loosened from effort, and the falchion seized
Easy was yielded.   Then the wroth king squeezed,
—Hurling the moon-disk of his shield afar,—
Him in both knotted arms of wiry war,
Rocked sidewise twice and thrice ;—as one hath
      seen
A stern wind take an ash-tree, roaring green,
Nodding its sappy bulk of trunk and boughs
To dizziness, from tough, coiled roots carouse
Its long height thundering ;—King Arthur shook
Sir Accolon and headlong flung.   Then took,
Tearing away, that scabbard from his side,
Flung through the breathless lists, that far and wide
Gulped in the battle voiceless.   Then right wroth
Secured Excalibur, and grasped of both
Wild hands swung glittering and brought bitter
      down
On rising Accolon.   Steel, bone and brawn
The blow hewed through.   Unsettled every sense,
Bathed in a world of blood, his limbs lay tense
And writhen, then ungathered limp with death.
Bent o'er him Arthur, from the brow beneath
Unlaced the helm and opened and then asked,
When the fair forehead's hair curled dark un-
      casqued :

"Say, ere thou diest, whence and what thou art!—
What king, what court is thine? And from what
    part
Of Britain dost thou come? Speak!—Yea, me-
    thinks
I have beheld thee—where? Before death drinks
The soul-light from life's cups, thine eyes . . .
    thou art—
What art thou, speak!"
                He answered, laboring short
With tortured breathing: "I?—one Accolon
Of Gaul—a knight of Arthur's court—at dawn—
God knows what I am now for love so slain!"
Then bent King Arthur nearer and again
Drew back; dim anguish in his manner, sighed:
"One of my own! one of my own! the pride
Of all my Table!"—Then asked softly, "Say,
Whose sword is this thou hadst, or in what way
Thou cam'st by it?" But, wandering, that knight
Heard with dull ears, divining but by sight
What had been asked, exclaimed, "Woe worth the
    sword!
—From love, thou hearest! yea, from love yet
    lord!—
From Morgane! lovely Morgane, who had made
Me strong o'er kings an hundred; to have swayed
Britain! hadst thou not risen like a fate
To make the world miscarry out of hate—
A king!—dost hear?—a gold and blood crowned
    king

With Arthur's sister-queen !—No bird can wing
Higher than her ambition, that resolved
King Arthur's death was needed ; and devolved
Plots that should prosper when the year grew sear,
Some liberal morning, like an almoner,
Prodigal of silver to the begging air ;
Some turbulent eve, that in heaven's turquoise
    rolled
Convulsive glories deep in fiery gold ;
Some night—the forest and the vasty night
Of summer stars—the king—the forest fight.—
Nay ! a crowned curse and crimeful clad she came
To me ; no woman, but a thing of flame,
That laughed on me with harlot lips that nursed
Death in wild kisses and the worm that cursed
My soul forever ! For, behind her youth,
She shrivels to a hag !—O vile untruth !—
Harlot !—nay, spouse of Urience, King of Gore !—
Sweet wanton !—nay, sweet death ! thou art not
    poor
In that thou hast thy dream, though love may
    grieve   .
That death so ruins it !—Thou dost perceive
How my soul hates thee !—Witness bear this field
How my soul loves thee !—What ! and will it
    yield ?—
Enough ! enough ! so hale me hence to die !"

Then anger in the good king's gloomy eye
Burnt, instant-embered, as one oft may see

A star leak out of heaven and cease to be.
Slow from his visage he his visor raised,
And on the dying one mute moment gazed,
Then grimly said, " Look on me ! Accolon,
I am that king !" He, with an awful groan,
Blade-battered as he was, beheld and knew ;
Strained to his tottering knees and haggard drew
Up full his armored height and hoarsely cried
" The king !" and at his mailed feet clashed and
    died. . . .

Then came a world of anxious faces, pressed
About King Arthur ; who, though sore distressed,
Bespake that multitude : " While breath and power
Remain, judge we these brothers : This harsh hour
Hath yielded Damas all this rich estate ;—
So it is his—allotted him by fate
And might of arms. So let it be to him.
For, stood our oath on knighthood not so slim
But that it hath this strong conclusiön.
This much by us as errant knight is done.—
Now our decree as King of Britain, hear :
We do adjudge Earl Damas banned fore'er,
Outlawed and exiled from all shores and isles
Of farthest Britain in its many miles.
One month be his, no more ! then will we come
Even with an iron host to seal his doom :
If he be not departed over seas,
Hang naked from his battlements t' appease
The wild hawks and of carrion-crows the craws.

Yea, we have said. . . . But all our favor
    draws
Toward Sir Ontzlake, whom it likes the king
To take into his knightly following.
He shall attend us homeward.   Ye have heard.—
But I am very weary.   Take my sword—
Unharness me ; for, battle-worn, I tire ;
And all my wounds are so much aching fire.
So, help me hence.   To-morrow we would fain
To Glastonbury and with us the slain."
So bare they then the wounded king away,
The dead behind, as closed the autumn day.

    .   .   .   .

But when within that abbey he grew strong,
The king, remembering the marauder wrong
Which Damas had inflicted on the land,
Commanded Lionell, with a staunch band,
To stamp this weed out if still rooted there.
He, riding thither to that robber lair,
Led Arthur's hopefulest helms, when, thorn on
    thorn
Reddened an hundred spears, one winter morn.
Built up, a bulk of bastioned rock on rock,
Vast battlements, that loomed above the shock
Of fighting foam that climbed with tearing hands,
Found cloudy-clustered turrets, in loud lands
Set desolate—mournful over frozen flats,—
Lone, hollow towers the haunt of owls and bats.

IV.

ENVIOUS and jealous of that high renown
    King Arthur had acquired for his crown,
Morgane rejoiced.—Knowing, though mightier
Than Accolon, without Excalibur,
Arthur, a stingless hornet, in the joust
Were less than dangerous. Confident, her trust
Smiled certain of conclusion ; eloquent,
Within her, whispered of success, that lent
Her heart a lofty hope ; and at large eyes
Piled up imperial dreams of power and prize.
And in her carven chamber, oaken-dark,
Traceried and arrased, o'er the barren park
That dripped with autumn,—for November lay
Swathed frostily in fog on every spray,—
Sate at her tri-arched casement, one wild night,
Ere yet came courier from that test of might ;
Her lord in slumber and the castle dull
With silence or of sad wind-music full :—

" Another monarch rises—Accolon !—
Love, Love with state more ermined ; balmy son
Of gods not men, and nobler hence to rule.
Sweet Love almighty, terrible to school
Harsh hearts to gentleness.—Then all this realm's
Iron-huskéd flower of war, which overwhelms
With rust and havoc, shall explode and bloom
An asphodel of peace with joy's perfume.
And then, O Launcelots and Tristrams, vowed

To Gueneveres and Isouds,—now allowed
No pleasures but what wary, stolen hours
In golden places have their flaming flowers,—
Ye shall have feasts of passion evermore !
Poor, out-thrust Love, now shivering at the door,
No longer, sweet neglected ! art thrust off,
Insulted and derided : nor the scoff
Of bully Power, whose heart of insult flings
Off for the roar of arms the appeal that clings
And lifts a tearful, prayerful, pitiful face
Up from his brutal feet : this shrine where grace
Lays woman's life for suffering sacrifice—
To him how little ! but of what pure price !
Her all, being all her all for love ! her soul,
Life, honor, earth and firmamental whole
Of God's glad universe : stars, moon and sun ;
Creation, death ; life ended, life begun.
And if by fleshly love all Heaven 's debarred,
Its sinuous, revolving spheres instarred,
Then Hell were Heaven with love to those who
        knew
Love which God's Heaven encouraged while it grew.

'' But this lank Urience who is my lord ?—
Why should I worry ? for, hath he no sword ?
No dangerous dagger I, hid softly here,
Sharp as an adder's fang ? or for that ear
No instant poison which insinuates,
Tightens quick pulses while the breath abates ?'' . . .
Thus had she then determined ; and the night

Sobbed on the towers, with no haggard, white
And watery moonbeam on the streaming pane,
But on the leads the soft, incessant rain,
A lamentable wind that wailed among
The turrets like a flying phantom throng.—

So grew her face severe as skies that take
Dark forces of some tragic storm and shake
With murmurous wrath black hills, and stab with
    fire
A pine the moaning forest mourns as sire ;
So touched her countenance that dark intent.
And to still eyes stern thoughts a passion sent
As midnight waters, luminous with deep
Suggestive worlds, glass austere stars in sleep,
Vague, ghostly gray locked in their hollow gloom.
Then as if some vast wind had swept the room,
Silent, intense, had raised her from her seat ;
Of dim, great arms had made her a retreat,
Secret as thought to move in ; like a ghost,
Noiseless as death and subtle as the frost,
Poised like a light and borne as carefully,
She trod the gusty hall where shadowy
The hangings rolled a dim Pendragon war.
And there the mail of Urience lay.   A star,
Glimmering above, a dying cresset dropped
From the stone vault and flared.   And here she
    stopped
And took the sword bright-burnished by his page
And ruddy as a flame with restless rage ;

For she had thought that, when they found him
    dead,
His sword laid by him on the bloody bed
Would be convictive that his own hand had
Done him this violence while fever-mad.
The sword she took ; and to the chamber, where
Her husband slept, she glided ; like an air
Twined in seductive sendal ; or a fit
Of faery song a wicked charm in it,
An incantation from the lips of death.
She paused beside his threshold ; for a breath
Listened ; and, sure he slept, stole in and stood
Dim by his couch.   About her heart the blood
Caught strangling, then throbbed thudding fever up
To her broad eyes, like wine whirled in a cup.

Then came rare Recollection, with a mouth
Sweet as the honeyed sunbeams of the South
Trickling through perplexed ripples of the leaves ;
To whose faint form a veil of starshine cleaves
Intricate gauze from memoried eyes to feet—
Feet sandaled with the sifted snows and fleet
To come and go and airy anxiously.
She, trembling to her, like a flower a bee
Nests in and makes an audible mouth of musk,
Dripping a downy language in the dusk,
Laid lips to ears and luted memories of
Now hated Urience :—Her maiden love,
That left Caerlleon willingly for Gore
One dazzling day of autumn.   How a boar,

Wild as the wonder of the blazing wood,
Raged at her from a cavernous solitude,
That, crimson-creepered, yawned the bristling
    curse
Murderous upon her. How her steed grew worse
And, terrified, fled snorting down the dell
Pursued with fear, and flung her from the selle,
Unhurt, upon a bank of springy moss,
That couched her swooning. In an utter loss
Of mind and limbs she only knew 't was thus—
As one who pants beneath an incubus :—
The boar thrust towards her a tusked snout and
    fanged
Of hideous bristles, and the whole wood clanged
And buzzed and boomed an hundred sounds and
    lights
Lawless about her brain, like leaves wild nights
Of hurricane harvest shouting. Then she knew
A fury thundered 'twixt them—and fleet flew
Rich-rooted moss and sandy loam that held
Dark-buried shadows of the wild, and swelled
Continual echoes with the thud of strife,
And breath of man and brute that warred for life ;
And all the air, made mad with foam and forms,
Spun froth and, 'twixt her, wrestled hair and arms,
While trampled caked the stricken leaves or, shred,
Hummed whirling, and snapped brittled branches
    dead.
And when she rose and leaned her throbbing head,
With all its uncoifed rays of raven hair

Disheveling shoulders pure and faultless fair,
On one milk, marvelous arm of fluid grace,
Beheld the brute thing throttled and the face
Of angry Urience over, browed like might,
One red swol'n arm, that pinned the hairy fright,
Strong as a god's, iron at the gullet's brawn ;
Dug in its midriff, the close knees updrawn
Wedged deep the glutton sides that quaked and
    strove
A shaggy bulk, whose sharp hoofs drove and drove.
Thus man and brute strained bent ; when Urience
    slipped
One arm, the horror's tearing tusks had ripped
And ribboned redly, to the dagger's hilt,
Which at his hip hung long a haft gold-gilt ;
Its rapid splinter drew ; beamed twice and thrice
High in the sun and, ghastly white as ice,
Plunged—and the great boar stretched in sullen
    death
Lay, in its harsh gorge bubbling blood and breath.

And how he brought her water from a well,—
A rustling freshness,—near them where it fell
From a moss-mantled rock, caught in his casque,
For her to drink ; then bathed her brow, a task
That had accompanying tears of joy and vows
Of love, sweet intercourse of eyes and brows,
And many clinging kisses eloquent.
And how, his wound dressed, she behind him bent
And clasped him on the same steed, and they went

On through the gold wood toward the golden west,
Till on one low hill's forest-covered crest
Up in the gold his castle's battlements pressed.
And then she felt she 'd loved him till had
    come
Fame of the love of Isoud, whom, from home,
Tristram had brought across the Irish foam ;
And Guenevere's for Launcelot of the Lake :
From these how her desire seemed to wake,
Longing for some great hero who would slake—
And such found Accolon.

                        And then she thought
How far she 'd fallen and how darkly fraught
With consequence was this. Then what distress
Were hers and his—her lover's, and success
How doubly difficult if, Arthur slain,
King Urience lived to assert his right to reign.
So she stood pondering with the sword ; her lips
Breathless and close, as her cold finger-tips
About the weapon's hilt. And so she sighed,
" Nay ! long, too long hast lived who shouldst have
    died
Even in the womb abortive ! who these years
Hast leashed my life to care with stinging tears,
A knot thus harshly severed !—As thou art
Into the elements naked ! "

                        O'er his heart
The long blade paused and—then descended hard.

Unfleshed, she laid it by her murdered lord ;
And the dark blood spread broader through the sheet
And dripped a horror at impassive feet,
And blurred the polished oak.   But lofty she
Stood proud, relentless ; in her ecstasy
A lovely devil ; a crowned lust that cried
On Accolon ; the rebel that defied
Control in all her senses ; clamorous as
Steep storm that down a cavernous mountain pass
Blasphemes an hundred echoes ; with like power
The inner wanton called its paramour ;   ·
Him whom, King Arthur had commanded, when
Borne from the lists, she should receive again
As his blithe gift and welcome from the joust,
For treacherous love and her more treacherous lust.

And while she stood revolving if her deed's
Secret were safe, behold ! a grind of steeds,
Arms and loud voices of fierce men that cursed
Coarse in the northern court.   To her athirst
For him her lover, war and power it spoke,
Him victor and so king.   And then awoke
A yearning to behold him ; and she fled
Like some wild specter down wide stairs, and red
Burst on a glare of links and glittering mail,
That shrunk her eyes and made her senses quail.
To her a bulk of iron, bearded fierce,
Down from a steaming steed into her ears,
" This from the King, O Queen ! " laughed harsh
        and hoarse :

Two henchmen beckoned, who pitched sheer with
    force,
Dull clanging at her feet, hacked, hewn, and red,
Crusted with blood, a knight in armor—dead ;
Her Accolon, flung with the mocking scoff
'' This from the King !''—phantoms in fog rode off.

     .   .   .   .   .   .

And what remains?—From Camelot to Gore
That night she weeping fled : thence to the shore,—
As that romancer tells,—Avilion,
Where she hath majesty gold-crowned and wan :
In darkest cypress a frail, piteous face
Queenly and lovely : 'round sad eyes the trace
Of immemorial tears as for some crime :
Eyes future-fixed, expectant of the time
When the forgiving Arthur cometh and
Shall have to rule all that lost golden land,
That drifts vague amber in forgotten seas
Of surgeless turquoise drowned in mysteries.—
Morgana, Queen of the gray Nevermore,
Who with crowned shadows out of Cornwall bore
The wounded Arthur from that last fought fight
Of Camlan in a black barge into night.
She who came wailing with a stately band
Of serge-stoled maidens from some far-off land
Of autumn-glimmer ; when were sharply strewn
The red leaves, and, broad o'er the hills, a moon
Swung full of frost a lustrous globe of gleams,
Faint on the mooning waves as shapes in dreams.

14

Epilogue.

FOR the mountains' hoarse greeting came hollow
      From stormy wind-chasms and caves ;
And I heard their wild cataracts wallow
      White bulks in long spasms of waves ;
And Merlin said, " Lo ! you must follow !
      And our path is o'er thousands of graves."

Then I felt that the black earth was porous
      And rotten with dust and with bones ;
And I knew that the ground that now bore us
      Was cadaverous with death as with stones ;
And I saw burning eyes, heard sonorous
      And dolorous gnashings and groans.

But the night of the tempest and thunder,
      The might of the terrible skies,
And the fire of Hell, that,—coiled under
      The hollow Earth,—smoulders and sighs,
And the laughter of stars and their wonder,
      Mingled and mixed in his eyes.

And we clomb—and the moon, old and sterile,
      Clomb with us o'er torrent and scar :
And I yearned towards her oceans of beryl,
      Wan mountains and cities of spar :
" 'T is not well," then he said, " you 're in peril
      Of falling and failing your star."

And we clomb—till we stood at the portal
  Of the uttermost point of the peak ;
And he led with a step more than mortal
  Far upward some presence to seek ;
And I felt that this love was immortal,
  This love, which had made me so weak.

We had clomb till the limbo of spirits
  Of darkness and crime deep below
Swung nebular ; nor could we hear its
  Lost wailing and clamor of woe,—
For we stood in a realm that inherits
  A vanquishing virgin of snow.

THE END.